# Ordinary Days In an Extraordinary Place

By A. J. Zeren

Ordinary Days In an Extraordinary Place


ISBN Information
Paperback ISBN 978-1-971684-00-0
Hardback ISBN 979-8-245363-38-7
Digital ISBN 978-1-971684-01-7

**To Asimov, Clarke, Vonnegut, Adams, Wells, Verne, and Bradbury**

# Table of Contents

## Sol 412

The seal was old. Not dangerously old—nothing on Mars was allowed to become that—but old in the way everything here aged: evenly, predictably, without complaint.

Evan Rourke floated a centimeter above the floor as he worked, boots hooked into the magnetic strip, one gloved hand braced against the bulkhead. The access panel had been opened so many times the screws had lost their individuality. He loosened them anyway, one by one, counting under his breath out of habit.

"Panel C, habitation ring, pressure seam four," he said into his recorder. "Routine inspection. Sol four-one-two. No visible deformation."

The recorder chimed softly. Logged.

Beyond the thin wall of composite alloy, Mars stretched outward—red, indifferent, perfect in its hostility. Evan didn't look at it. He had learned early on that looking too long made you start thinking in the wrong directions.

The seal came free with a faint sigh, like a tired animal finally allowed to rest. He peeled it back, examined the edges, ran a gloved finger along the inner lip.

Still elastic. Still compliant. Still doing its job.

"Minor abrasion on inner rim," he continued. "Within tolerance. Replacing as scheduled."

The words felt good in his mouth. Within tolerance. As scheduled. Proof that the universe was behaving.

He clipped the old seal to his belt and reached for the replacement. Fresh polymer, faintly blue, smelling faintly of nothing. Everything on Mars smelled like nothing, unless something had gone wrong. Smells were warnings here, not comforts.

As he worked, his mind drifted—not to Earth, not anymore, but to the checklist. The checklist was a kind of prayer. Each item acknowledged, each task completed, a small affirmation that the day would proceed as it should.

Seal seated. Pressure test nominal.

"Panel C resealed," he said. "No anomalies."

The recorder chimed again.

Evan exhaled and unhooked his boots, letting himself drift back to the floor. Artificial gravity caught him gently. He stood there for a moment longer than necessary, hand resting against the wall, feeling the faint vibration of the habitat's systems running beneath his palm.

Alive, he thought. Still alive.

The corridor outside was quiet in the way Mars favored: no incidental noise, no background clutter. Every sound meant something. The soft hum of air circulation. The distant whine of a rover returning to dock. Footsteps, when there were footsteps, echoed slightly too long.

Evan sealed his kit and pushed off toward the commons.

Breakfast was rehydrated eggs and protein grain, yellow and beige in careful balance. He ate at the long table beneath the LED skylight that mimicked a pale blue Earth morning. The light cycle said it was early. His body agreed, mostly.

Across from him, Mei Torres scrolled through a tablet, brow furrowed.

"Morning," Evan said.

She looked up, blinked, then smiled. "Morning. You're early."

"Seal inspection," he said. "Panel C."

She grimaced. "That one again?"

"Everything again," Evan said, and they both smiled, because that was funny in a way that didn't require much effort.

Mei tapped her tablet. "Comms is running slow today."

"Slow how?"

She shrugged. "Latency spikes. Packet loss. Nothing serious."

Nothing serious was the phrase of the colony. Nothing serious meant the problem had been acknowledged, classified, and deprioritized.

"Dust?" Evan asked.

"Probably," Mei said. "It's always dust."

Mars found its way into everything eventually. Filters, joints, thoughts.

They ate in companionable silence for a while. Evan watched the simulated sky slowly brighten, the programmed sun climbing a fraction higher. He knew exactly how many LEDs were in that panel. He'd helped install them.

"Storm’s coming," Mei said eventually. "Southern hemisphere. Big one."

"Always is," Evan replied.

She hesitated, then lowered her voice. "You heard anything from Earth?"

The question landed softly, but it landed.

Evan didn't look at her. He kept his eyes on his tray, on the way the rehydrated eggs had pooled slightly at the edge.

"No," he said. "Why would I?"

She shrugged again, but this one was tighter. "Just... wondering."

He nodded. "Comms backlog. Happens."

"Yeah," she said. "Happens."

They both knew the lie, but it was a small one, and practiced. Lies on Mars weren't about deception. They were about smoothing edges.

After breakfast, Evan headed to the observation blister—not to observe, really, but to log the dust accumulation on the exterior panels. The storm was still distant, a faint smear on the horizon, but the sensors were already reporting increased particulate density. He keyed in the numbers, watching the curve climb exactly as predicted.

"Incremental increase," he murmured. "Within tolerance."

Everything was within tolerance today.

The Earth window sat dark at the edge of the blister, its status light steady amber. Not green. Not red. Amber meant pending. Amber meant waiting.

Evan stared at it for a moment longer than he should have.

"Not now," he told himself quietly, and turned away.

The day unfolded as it always did. Maintenance rounds. System checks. A brief meeting in Habitat Control where Administrator Kessler reminding them—again—about water conservation targets, as if any of them had forgotten.

"We're exceeding projections," Kessler said, smiling thinly. "Good work."

Good work. Evan wrote it down in his notebook, even though he didn't need to. Writing made it real.

At midday, the storm arrived.

The sky darkened, red deepening to something almost purple as the dust thickened. The habitat lights compensated automatically, brightening by imperceptible degrees. Evan watched the adjustment happen, felt a small, irrational relief at the smoothness of it.

The storm pressed against the dome, grains of ancient rock hissing softly as they slid and scraped. Mars reminding them it was there.

"Still within tolerance," Evan said to no one.

In the afternoon, the Earth window chimed.

It was a soft sound, easily missed. Evan almost did miss it, focused as he was on recalibrating a sensor array. The second chime caught his attention.

Amber blinking.

He froze.

The protocol said wait. Protocol said finish the task at hand, log the anomaly, proceed in order. Evan closed his eyes for a moment, then saved his work and pushed off toward the comms station.

The room was empty when he arrived. The display glowed faintly, lines of code scrolling beneath the amber indicator.

"Comms," he said. "Status?"

No automated response. That was new.

"Comms," he repeated, more sharply. "Status report."

The amber light pulsed once, then steadied.

Evan swallowed.

He opened the diagnostics panel. The data streamed in: signal strength nominal. Receiver functioning. Transmission queue empty.

Empty.

"That's not right," he whispered.

He checked the timestamp on the last received packet.

Sol 410. Early.

Two days ago.

Evan's heart thudded in his chest. He forced himself to breathe slowly, evenly, the way they taught during emergency drills.

"Okay," he said out loud. "Okay."

He ran a deeper scan. No hardware faults. No software errors. The system was ready, waiting.

Waiting for something that wasn't coming.

"Dust," he said automatically. "It's the storm."

But even as he said it, he knew. Dust didn't do this. Dust degraded signals, it introduced noise. Dust didn't erase them cleanly.

Footsteps echoed in the corridor. Mei appeared in the doorway, eyes flicking immediately to the console.

"You got it too," she said.

Evan nodded. "Last packet was Sol 410."

Her jaw tightened. "That's... longer than usual."

"Yeah."

They stood there, side by side, staring at the amber light. It felt like staring at a closed door, knowing no one was on the other side.

"Should we call Kessler?" Mei asked.

Evan hesitated. The protocol said yes. Protocol said escalate anomalies beyond twenty-four hours.

Protocol also said panic was the enemy.

"Let's run another check," he said. "Just to be sure."

They ran it together, fingers flying over the interface with practiced ease. The results didn't change.

Silence, rendered in numbers.

Mei leaned back, exhaling sharply. "Earth's gone quiet before."

"Not like this," Evan said.

Another pause. Longer this time.

"What if it's just... a delay?" she said. "Some rerouting. Solar interference."

Evan wanted to believe her. He wanted to latch onto the idea and not let go.

"Within tolerance," he said instead, because that was what you said when you didn't know what else to say.

They logged the anomaly. They forwarded it to Kessler with careful wording, stripping it of any emotional weight.

Extended communication delay. Cause undetermined. Monitoring.

The amber light continued to blink.

The rest of the day passed in a haze. Evan moved through his tasks on muscle memory alone, hands steady even as his thoughts drifted.

Earth is silent.

He tried to imagine it—billions of people, cities, oceans—all suddenly... what? Quiet? Broken? Gone?

The thought slid off his mind, unable to find purchase. It was too big, too abstract. Mars had trained him out of that kind of thinking.

At dinner, the commons were louder than usual. Not panicked—just talkative, voices overlapping slightly more than normal.

"Probably a storm," someone said.

"Solar flare," another offered.

"Maintenance on the relay," Kessler said, projecting calm like a shield.

Evan ate, nodded, laughed at the right moments. He didn't mention the timestamp again.

Later, alone in his quarters, he opened his personal log.

Sol 412, he wrote. Routine maintenance completed. All systems are normal.

His fingers hovered over the keyboard.

He thought about adding something else. About the amber light. About the quiet.

He didn't.

He closed the log and lay back on his bunk, staring at the ceiling. The habitat hummed around him, steady and reliable.

Mars didn't care if Earth was listening.

Tomorrow, the seal on Panel D would need inspection. The storm would pass. The dust would settle.

Life would continue.

And for the first time, Evan understood that that was the most frightening possibility of all.

## The Quietest Signal

Marisol Vega sat at the communications console in the northern wing of the habitat, fingers poised above the touchpad as though she could summon a reply with intention alone. Her boots were anchored into the floor, though she didn't need them yet—the slight artificial gravity kept her body weight honest, balanced. The room smelled faintly of ozone and the recycled air of Mars, sterile but intimate in its regularity.

She had been awake for hours, longer than anyone else, listening to static. Endless, unchanging, neutral static that arrived in rhythmic pulses. There was no panic in the station—none should be—but there was curiosity, and that was almost as dangerous.

She touched a soft icon on the pad. The static shifted subtly. Tiny fluctuations, patterns she had traced countless times. They were meaningless. Yet somehow meaningful.

"Morning, Marisol," a voice said. She didn't turn immediately.

"Morning, Jiro," she replied softly, fingers still poised.

He appeared in the doorway, a mess of hair sticking to the edge of his visor. He looked human enough, but Mars had a way of sculpting people differently—longer fingers, leaner faces, eyes always slightly squinting, as if squinting at some invisible horizon.

"You've been here a while," he said.

"Since the storm," Marisol replied. That was true, at least. The southern tempest had kicked up dust that clogged the solar arrays and delayed some communication bursts. "Static doesn't care about storms," she added, almost reflexively.

Jiro leaned against the doorway, arms crossed. "And you care?"

Marisol hesitated. The question had no weight on Earth, but here it carried gravity. A signal might mean nothing—but ignoring it could be catastrophic if it meant something.

"I care enough to know it isn't nothing," she said.

He nodded, then gestured at the screens. "I've run the diagnostics twice this morning. Hardware is fine. Receivers are fine. Transmission queues are empty."

"Empty," Marisol echoed, softly.

She ran a hand along the edge of the console, feeling the cool polymer beneath her glove. Empty was familiar. Mars had taught her to trust that the absence of a signal was sometimes more informative than the signal itself.

"You think it's Earth?" Jiro asked cautiously.

Marisol shook her head, then realized she did not know why she shook her head. She paused, listening to the rhythm of the pulsing static. It seemed to breathe along with her own heartbeat.

"Maybe," she said finally.

They didn't need to speak louder than that. Words on Mars were only half the communication. The rest was posture, pause, and presence.

For hours, they worked quietly, side by side. Jiro scrolled through logs, Marisol adjusted filters, tweaked frequencies. Each adjustment had a purpose, a name, a sequence. The colony thrived on sequences, on procedures. Procedure was the only thing that outlasted doubt.

During a brief break, they sat on a bench against the wall, visors lifted, revealing flushed faces and damp hair. Outside the windows, the storm's edges softened, leaving the landscape a uniform, ochre calm.

"You ever think about Earth?" Jiro asked, voice hesitant.

Marisol didn't answer immediately. Thinking about Earth here was like holding a candle against the sun: the more she tried, the less she saw.

"Sometimes," she said finally. "But thinking doesn't change the signal."

"Not yet," he said.

They shared a faint laugh. Mars had a way of drawing out humor, fragile and thin, yet precious. Humor wasn't abundant—it was a lubricant that kept them from sticking too firmly to despair.

Back at the console, the day passed with a rhythm that was almost meditative. Static. Diagnostics. Logs. Repeats. Minor adjustments. Everything within tolerance.

Then it happened. The first anomaly.

Marisol noticed a subtle shift in the pulse, almost imperceptible if not for the hours she had spent memorizing its cadence. A single blip, perfectly placed between the monotony. She froze, gloved fingers hovering.

"Did you see that?" she whispered.

Jiro leaned over, scanning the same display. "Probably just interference," he said.

But Marisol couldn't dismiss it. She watched the pulse again, then another, then another. Patterns emerging. Tiny, deliberate, almost intentional.

"Someone's trying to communicate," she said softly.

Jiro's brow furrowed. "Or... we're reading it wrong."

She shook her head. "No. Not this time. Not today."

A tension settled over the station, subtle but thick, like dust before a storm. Neither of them spoke for a while, letting the anomaly pulse across the screen. Every beat carried both promise and threat.

"You should report this," Jiro said finally.

Marisol considered the implications. Reporting meant involving others, triggering protocols, potentially sending them into a spiral they weren't equipped to manage.

"Or I could..." she trailed off.

"You could what?"

"Do nothing," she said. "Just monitor. See where it goes."

Jiro studied her for a long moment, then nodded slowly. It was a quiet act of rebellion—not against Mars, but against the weight of expectation. Sometimes the weight itself was the most dangerous gravity.

By mid-afternoon, they had mapped the pulse into a readable format, noting subtle variations that suggested intelligence, purpose, maybe even intent. The patterns didn't promise survival or catastrophe. They promised... observation.

"Do you think they're... alive?" Jiro asked quietly, almost afraid of the answer.

Marisol exhaled slowly, fingers tracing the surface of the console. "Alive? Maybe. Or maybe they just wait. Silence is a form of control too."

Jiro's hands flexed, unconsciously mimicking her gesture. They were silent for a long while, letting the pulse fill the space between them. No words could translate what they were feeling, but the quiet sufficed. Mars was generous that way—its quiet was a companion.

As the habitat lights shifted with the artificially controlled day, the pulse persisted, a steady, deliberate heartbeat beneath their own. Marisol leaned back in her chair, letting herself feel the faint rush of something she hadn't felt in months: anticipation.

"Do you think anyone on Earth even knows we're here?" Jiro asked.

Marisol considered it. The pulse didn't answer, but it didn't need to.

"Doesn't matter," she said finally. "Not for us. Not today."

The hours passed. The storm faded. The pulse remained, steady, almost comforting in its constancy. They monitored, noted, cataloged. Everything was within tolerance, and yet, something was changing. The colony itself felt different, as if the signal—tiny, patient, persistent—was an observer, a presence in their lives they couldn't name but could feel.

Dinner was silent. Both of them ate mechanically, utensils scraping against trays. Words felt unnecessary, almost intrusive. They communicated through presence, through the shared awareness of that steady pulse.

Later, Marisol returned to the console alone. She ran a deeper diagnostic, checked the logs one more time. Everything was nominal. Everything was within tolerance.

And yet, she stayed. Because the pulse, whatever it was, demanded attention. Not panic, not action. Just notice. A recognition of the quiet truth that they were not alone, even if Earth had gone silent.

By the time artificial night settled over the habitat, Marisol leaned back, staring at the amber light on the console. It blinked with deliberate slowness, a small rhythm against the larger heartbeat of the colony.

She closed her eyes, letting herself breathe with it.

Mars didn't need her to act.

The signal didn't need her to understand.

She simply existed, and that was enough for today.

And for the first time, Marisol felt a kind of kinship with something vast, unknowable, patient, and unseen. Something that watched quietly, not out of malice or care, but because it could.

And the silence, for once, was not empty.

# Dust accumulation Log

Riley Chen's day began before the sun simulation even reached its midpoint. The habitat lights hummed awake, pale white filling the corridors, and Riley, like all of them, rose obediently to the rhythm of habit. Outside, Mars stretched in endless shades of ochre and crimson, dust motes catching the faint light of the distant sun. Riley didn't look. They had learned long ago that looking too long invited questions that had no answers.

Today's task was simple, repetitive, yet crucial: measure dust accumulation on the solar arrays, record the data, repeat. Every sol, every panel, every micron counted. It wasn't glamorous. It wasn't heroic. But in the quiet order of Mars, it was survival.

**Panel A1: 0.5 microns.**

**Panel A2: 0.6 microns.**

**Panel A3: 0.7 microns.**

Riley typed carefully, noting the minor increases. Then paused, fingers hovering. They remembered yesterday's entry differently than the log recorded. Panel A3 had been 0.6 yesterday. Or 0.7. Something about the number didn't align with memory. It was subtle—almost imperceptible—but it planted unease.

They shook it off and moved to Panel B1. 1.1 microns. Within tolerance. Fine. Reliable. Predictable.

Dust was comforting that way. Dust didn't lie. Dust didn't forget.

Still, Riley scribbled a note in the margin of the log: Did I measure this correctly?

It was a private note, meaningless to anyone but themselves. In that, there was intimacy. It was the closest they had to conversation.

By mid-morning, Riley had been joined by Tev, a systems technician. Tev crouched over the array maintenance screen, stylus tapping lightly against the glass.

"Morning," Tev said.

Riley nodded. "Panel B3 is marginally higher than expected. Wind shifts, I guess."

Tev leaned back, gaze drifting to the viewport. "You ever notice how dust covers everything equally? Doesn't care if it's a panel or your boots."

Riley smiled faintly. "Equal opportunity annoyance."

Tev chuckled, soft, and for a moment the day felt lighter. Humor on Mars was rare, fragile, like ice underfoot.

"I miss the rain," Tev said suddenly. The words surprised Riley. Not because they weren't true, but because they weren't often spoken. Rain was an idea, a memory of Earth's intimacy, the way water moved and reshaped everything.

Riley considered that. "I miss... not knowing dust this intimately," they said finally.

Tev laughed again. "Fair."

The moment passed. Routine reclaimed the room like a tide. Riley returned to the measurements, Tev to diagnostics. The panels hummed under their attention. Dust continued to accumulate at its slow, steady pace.

**Panel C2: 0.9 microns.**

**Panel C3: 1.0 microns.**

Numbers, neutral and indifferent. They told the truth in ways human memory couldn't.

Lunch was mechanical. Riley ate with the log open, fingers tapping the screen, mind elsewhere. They remembered meals differently each day: yesterday's taste, today's texture, tomorrow's meal, all blurring together. Memory eroded on Mars in small increments. It wasn't dramatic. It was subtle, insidious.

After lunch, a storm began in the distance, a gentle swell at first, then a quiet roar, sand and dust rising to meet the thin sky. Riley walked to the observation deck, Tev following silently.

"You ever think," Tev began, voice hesitant, "that maybe we'll forget Earth entirely?"

Riley considered it. "I think we already have," they said. Not as a prediction, but as observation. Every detail of Mars pressed itself into them, replacing the soft, fading contours of memory.

Tev shivered, not from cold, but from recognition. "That... that's scary."

Riley nodded. "Scary is different than harmful."

They watched the dust swirl against the reinforced glass, a storm contained, predictable, yet alive in its own way. The wind carried no messages, only weight. Yet the panels outside were affected. Every micron of dust added was a small, inexorable claim.

Back at the log, Riley noticed something odd. Panel D1: 0.8 microns. Yesterday it was 0.8 microns. Today... 0.7?

Impossible.

They double-checked. Measurements, instruments, calculations. All consistent.

And yet the number had decreased.

Riley's pulse quickened slightly. Errors happened. Dust shifted, wind carried it. But Mars didn't lie. Not really. Not intentionally.

They made a note: Recheck tomorrow.

The day progressed, ritual after ritual, calculation after calculation. Tev had gone to check air filtration, Riley returned to recording data. Every micron measured, every log entry made, felt simultaneously trivial and sacred.

**Panel E3: 1.2 microns.**

**Panel E4: 1.3 microns.**

Numbers steady again. Predictable. Reassuring.

Riley's mind wandered to memory again. The day they had first arrived on Mars. The excitement of descent, the awe, the fear. Those emotions were still accessible, but thinner now, like distant radio signals, faint and crackling.

And then, as if acknowledging Riley's thought, the dust accumulation chart on their screen shifted ever so slightly. A pattern. A rhythm. Subtle, almost imperceptible.

They leaned closer. Was it a measurement error, a sensor drift... or something else?

The thought made the hair on the back of Riley's neck prickle. Mars didn't often make them question themselves. Routine didn't. Dust didn't. But the numbers—themselves objective, impartial—had changed in a way that defied expectation.

By evening, Riley had closed the log for the day, entries complete, margins filled with small personal annotations. Notes of doubt, observations, questions about what they had seen or remembered.

They left the observation deck, moving slowly through the corridor as artificial night settled over the habitat. The storm had passed. Dust floated in suspended streams beneath the lights. Everything was calm. Everything within tolerance.

Tev passed them in the hall, pausing. "You okay?"

Riley nodded. "Better than okay. Alive. Panels within tolerance."

Tev smiled faintly. "Good enough, then."

Riley pressed their gloved hand to the wall as they passed, feeling the hum of the life-support systems beneath. It was comforting. Solid. The kind of presence Mars offered when no other did.

Later, alone, Riley returned to the log. They scrolled through the day's measurements. Everything was clean, precise. Ordered. Logical. And yet, there was unease. Something in the data shifted, something that couldn't be explained. A tiny imperfection in the perfection of routine.

They stared at it. Not fear, exactly. Not curiosity, exactly. Just awareness.

Mars had a way of reminding you that you were small. That your life, your memory, your humanity was fragile. And yet, it continued—unchanged, impervious, indifferent.

Riley leaned back, letting themselves breathe, letting the small hum of the habitat fill the empty spaces inside them. Numbers could be trusted. Dust could be trusted. Routine could be trusted.

And for now, that was enough.

Even if something was changing beneath it all, something subtle, patient, inexorable.

The dust would cover it eventually.

And tomorrow, they would measure again.

## The longest morning

Kai Harrington woke to the hum of the habitat's systems like a heartbeat that wasn't his own. The artificial gravity tugged gently at his legs as he floated upright, boots locking automatically into the floor. He glanced at the LED clock above the door: 0600, Sol 418.

Or was it Sol 418?

He rubbed his eyes. The numbers hadn't changed since yesterday, or maybe yesterday was two hours ago, or two days. Time had a way of folding here, slipping under the skin until it became something elastic, impossible to measure.

Kai ran his hand along the edge of his bunk, feeling the familiar grooves worn into the surface. These grooves were small, human-scale proofs that someone had been here before him, and they comforted him. Or perhaps unsettled him—they were proof that continuity existed, even if he could no longer trust the days themselves.

Breakfast was the usual: rehydrated oatmeal, thick and grainy, with a smear of preserved fruit paste. The usual smells, the usual textures, and yet, somehow, they tasted different every time he ate them.

Kai's roommate, Luma, appeared in the doorway, blinking against the light. Her hair was tied back in a messy braid, flecks of dust clinging to the ends.

"You up early... or late?" she asked.

Kai shrugged. "Time is flexible," he said, then realized the words sounded hollow.

They ate in silence, listening to the soft whirring of air circulation. Outside, the morning sun simulated across the viewport, pale and unreal, painting the Martian ground in muted shades of red.

Kai stood after a few bites and pushed off to the geology lab, grav boots securing him against the floor. Today's task: surveying a mineral vein near the northern ridge. Sensors and drones had mapped it weeks ago, but human eyes were still required. Routine. Procedure. Kai could follow it without thinking.

But when he stepped into the lab, the computer terminal was flickering, showing data that conflicted with yesterday's readings. The vein had shifted. Slightly, almost imperceptibly, but enough to make him pause.

He double-checked the coordinates. The same. The sensors. The same.

And yet, the vein had moved.

He frowned, tapping at the interface, pulling up historical logs. Each scan was identical—until it wasn't. Then suddenly, the numbers snapped back to match the previous day.

Kai leaned back in his chair, breath catching. His hands trembled slightly as he scrolled again. Nothing had changed. And yet, he remembered the change.

"Hey," Luma said from the doorway, voice cautious. "You okay?"

Kai blinked. "I... I think I've seen this before."

She frowned. "Seen what?"

"The vein," he said. "The map... it shifted. Or maybe it didn't. I can't tell."

Luma approached, touching his arm lightly. "Maybe it's just a glitch. The computers do that sometimes."

Kai shook his head. "It's not a glitch. I... I remember it differently."

She didn't press him further. On Mars, memory was a fragile, private thing. You learned not to question it too loudly.

The morning stretched on. Kai checked and rechecked the mineral vein, running scans, examining rock formations with tactile sensors. Each reading confirmed the previous. Each observation contradicted what he remembered.

By midday, his frustration had mounted. He stepped outside the habitat into the thin Martian air, visor sealed, boots sinking slightly into the loose regolith. He stared at the ridge. The sun was shifting faster than expected—or was it slower? He couldn't tell.

A drone floated near him, hovering in silence, recording. He had sent these devices out hundreds of times, but today they felt different, like witnesses to something beyond measurement.

He bent to inspect the vein manually, brushing regolith aside. It was exactly as it had been yesterday. And yet, he remembered the vein differently.

A sudden gust of wind stirred the dust around him, sharp and abrasive. It was not dangerous—but it caught his visor, streaking the glass with fine particles. He shook his head, wiped the view, and squinted.

Something flickered in the corner of his vision. Movement? Shadow? No—nothing there. Just dust. Always dust.

But the unease had taken root.

Kai returned to the habitat, tracking every step with meticulous logs, trying to anchor himself in sequence, in procedure. The day had become a loop, a folding hour, and he knew that any mistake in logging could unravel it further.

Luma met him at the lab doorway, carrying a tray of rehydrated noodles. "You've been out there a while," she said, worry sharpening her tone. "You've eaten? Hydrated?"

Kai nodded. "Yes," he said, then hesitated. "No. I don't... I'm not sure anymore."

She looked at him, silent, empathetic, waiting without pushing. Kai realized in that moment that someone noticing, someone simply being present, was more grounding than any data readout.

They sat together at a workstation, logging observations. Minutes felt like hours, hours like minutes. Each tick of the simulated clock mocked him.

Kai began to notice subtle discrepancies: Luma's handwriting yesterday—was it slightly different today? The screensaver wallpaper—did he change it, or did it change itself?

By mid-afternoon, he had begun running mental simulations, retracing the past hours over and over. Nothing was consistent. And yet, the habitat, the colony, the dust outside—the physical, unyielding world—was stable, reliable.

"Maybe," he said aloud, "Mars doesn't care if we remember or not."

Luma nodded. "Indifference is a constant here," she said quietly. "We adapt. Or we fade."

Kai shivered, not from cold, but from understanding. Mars wasn't hostile. It didn't need to be. It merely existed, vast and eternal, and the humans were incidental, like echoes in a canyon that would slowly erase itself if no one listened.

The afternoon brought a minor systems anomaly. A small power fluctuation in the lab. Protocol demanded investigation. Kai and Luma traced it to a dust build-up in a minor conduit. Nothing catastrophic. Nothing urgent.

And yet, the mundane act of clearing the dust, recalibrating the system, following procedure, became a tether to sanity. Every screw tightened, every panel inspected, every log entry saved, anchored Kai in a reality that seemed to be folding around him.

By the time the simulated sun reached the "evening" threshold, Kai realized he could no longer remember why he had wanted to return to Earth at all. The thought had existed in his mind hours ago—or days ago—but now it was slippery, intangible.

Luma noticed the look on his face. "You're thinking about home," she said gently.

Kai shook his head. "No. Not thinking. Forgetting."

They didn't speak for a long while. The habitat lights dimmed, the artificial evening stretching longer than the natural rhythm. Outside, the red dust glimmered faintly in the last light, unmoving, indifferent.

Kai sat on a bench, watching the ridge, listening to the faint hum of the colony. The world felt smaller, yet infinitely larger. Time itself seemed to stretch, looping, folding back onto itself.

By the time Kai finally lay down, exhaustion claimed him—not from labor, but from perception. He had lived an entire day, or perhaps a fraction of it, or perhaps an echo of several days. He could not say.

Mars had made him forget.

And yet, in the quiet, the pulse of the colony, the presence of Luma, and the simple certainty of the habitat's hum, Kai felt a fragile, stubborn flicker of self remain.

The longest morning had ended, though no one could tell where it had begun.

Tomorrow, or the day after, or the day before—it didn't matter. Kai would rise again. Procedure would continue. Dust would accumulate. Observations would be made.

Mars didn't care.

But somehow, somehow, so did he.

## Red Sky, Silent Storm

Kaelen Mira adjusted the calibration on the anemometer, the faint hum of the instrument echoing softly in the observation dome. The early sol light fell in muted angles across the red plains, filtered through the thick, dusty atmosphere. Outside, the wind traced invisible paths across ridges and craters, stirring fine particles into lazy, twisting eddies. The colony's systems hummed beneath her feet, vibrating through the steel floor in quiet rhythms, a heartbeat without urgency.

She tapped the console, pulling up the day's atmospheric projections. The models were all in agreement: today would be calm. Calm, by Martian standards. Wind speeds measured in barely perceptible meters per second. Dust devils, if they formed, would be small, transient, harmless. The sensors confirmed it: nothing in the sky, nothing in the soil, nothing in the far horizon demanded attention.

And yet, Kaelen felt the old reflex—an urge to anticipate, to expect the sudden, to wait for the unexpected. Earth had trained her for storms that struck without warning, for chaos that tore down walls and demanded action. But here, on Mars, the storms were patient. Indifferent. Silent.

A faint rattle drifted through the dome. She traced it to the exterior vent flaps, vibrating gently in the low wind. The sound was mundane, almost comforting, a reminder that the planet moved regardless of human observation. Still, her fingers hovered over the console, ready to amplify, analyze, record, react.

Minutes stretched. The sun climbed higher, its light weak and pink, illuminating the ridges in soft relief. Dust motes hung in the beams, drifting like tiny galaxies. Kaelen exhaled slowly, feeling the weight of anticipation recede and then return in cycles. The colony thrived in precision; every sensor, every log, every drone patrolled exactly as programmed. Yet she could not shake the sensation that the planet was holding something back.

She opened the projection feed and swept the digital horizon, watching the wind patterns trace gentle arcs across valleys. There it was—a faint spiral, a dust devil forming quietly in the distance. Not threatening, not fast, not violent, just... there. Its motion was hypnotic, elegant in its slow dance. Kaelen watched it for minutes, noting its path, speed, and height. She could predict it almost perfectly with her models, yet her pulse quickened slightly, the human reflex to observe and anticipate refusing to quiet.

"Beautiful," she whispered, more to herself than to anyone else.

A voice interrupted. "Kaelen." Marcus leaned against the doorway, his arms folded. His eyes followed the same faint spiral curling across the plains. "It doesn't need us, does it?"

"No," Kaelen said softly. "It doesn't." She returned her gaze to the dust devil, marveling at the simplicity of its existence. It neither feared nor acknowledged the colony. It did not need her observations, her models, her simulations. It was perfect in its indifference.

Marcus nodded. "We've been monitoring this for sols now. Same pattern. Predictable. Harmless. And yet... every time it forms, we check, log, calibrate. We act as though it matters."

Kaelen smiled faintly, a mixture of amusement and melancholy. "Because it used to matter. On Earth, the wind could kill. The storm could collapse a building or wash away a field. Here, it teaches patience. Observation. Detachment. But still... our instincts remain."

She returned to the console, adjusting sensor parameters to track the tiny particles swirling in the eddy. Even in this low-stakes simulation, she felt the familiar tension: will the formation hold, will it fade, will it surprise her? And then the reality settled like dust in the calm air: nothing will happen. The planet does not need to challenge her. Humans alone create the anticipation, the drama, the stakes.

By midday, the dust devil had dissipated, curling into nothingness like smoke in a faint breeze. Kaelen logged its metrics, then watched a second form begin to take shape farther away, smaller, less defined. She could trace its path mathematically, estimate its decay, predict its dissolution. Yet she could not shake the feeling that she was watching something alive, something indifferent, something that existed without her observation yet still pulled at the human need to witness.

She walked toward the habitat's edge, looking out at the plain. Engineers and technicians moved between modules, calibrating, checking, recording—every movement precise, predictable, human in its routine. The children played nearby, floating in low gravity, inventing games from shadows and light, their laughter unfamiliar and fragile against the backdrop of an uncaring planet.

Kaelen paused. She considered the contrast: human life, vibrant, adaptive, unpredictable, performing within exacting routines; Mars, vast, patient, silent, moving according to its own rules. A slow realization sank in: the planet could teach without force, shape without interference, observe without judgment. Its indifference was the highest form of discipline.

She returned to the console, amplifying minor wind fluctuations, simulating patterns, running predictive models. Each calculation confirmed her own observations: nothing unexpected would occur. No storm would breach the colony's walls. No gust would damage equipment. No dust devil would challenge the routines of life here.

And yet, as she watched the data, she felt a strange satisfaction. Not triumph. Not relief. Something quieter. Recognition. Understanding. Humanity persisted, but so did the planet's autonomy. Life had meaning only because humans assigned it. Mars was beautiful, terrifying, instructive, indifferent—and utterly patient.

Hours passed. She recorded the final readings of the sol, each entry meticulous, exact, flawless. The dust spirals had come and gone. Wind speeds remained constant. Temperatures shifted predictably. Solar intensity was low, gentle, and steady. Every system thrived. Every routine persisted. Humans thrived within them.

As the sun dipped toward the horizon, scattering faint light across the ridges and valleys, Kaelen stepped outside into the filtered airlock. The planet stretched endlessly, scarlet and gold and orange, moving without regard. She inhaled deeply, the recycled oxygen carrying the faint metallic tang of habitat filtration. For a moment, she let herself imagine the wind could speak, could care, could demand. It did not. She smiled at the truth of it.

Marcus joined her on the observation deck. "You're calm," he said, noting the serenity in her posture.

Kaelen turned to him. "I am. There is nothing to fear. Nothing to fight. Nothing to save." She gestured at the plains. "Mars does not care.

It is patient. It teaches only through observation. And we... we continue."

He nodded, quiet for a long moment. "And that's enough?"

Kaelen considered him, then smiled faintly. "It must be. It is all we have. And perhaps that is all we need."

The dust swirled again, faint, delicate, infinite. The colony hummed below, alive with precise routines. Children laughed, engineers calibrated, medics recorded, teachers guided. Life moved, human and imperfect in its spirit, perfect in its execution.

Kaelen returned inside, closing the airlock. She made her final log entry for the sol:

"The storm never arrived. The wind moved without notice. Life persisted perfectly. We survived, but we did not struggle. Humanity thrives, yet remains alien to itself. Mars watches. We exist. That is all. That is enough."

She powered down the observation systems, letting the artificial nightfall dim the habitat lights. Outside, the planet rotated in patient silence. The dust motes drifted, spiral upon spiral, obeying no command, no calculation, no observer.

Kaelen Mira settled into her chair, letting the hum of the colony wash over her. Perfection. Silence. Indifference. The storm never came. And in that absence, in that quiet, she found an almost unbearable clarity: humanity's endurance did not require struggle. It required only observation, persistence, and the acceptance of a world that neither needed nor noticed it.

The last storm had passed.

And Mars continued, exactly as it always had, perfectly indifferent, perfectly patient, perfectly eternal.

## Borrowed gravity

Dr. Anya Patel adjusted the harness straps across her shoulders, feeling the subtle pull of Mars' gravity on her chest, her spine, and her bones. She had worn this suit every sol for the past six months, measuring muscle tone, bone density, and cardiovascular response. Each reading had been predictable. Each adaptation is documented meticulously. Each anomaly noted, logged, and filed away.

Yet today felt different.

The morning began quietly, with the usual protocol. The physiologist's lab smelled faintly of synthetic rubber, antiseptic wipes, and the subtle tang of recycled air. Machines hummed as they always did, steady and insistent, indifferent. Anya greeted her colleagues with polite nods, noting the slight lag in their reflexes caused by low gravity. Small deviations, barely perceptible, but all cataloged and stored.

"Morning, Ezra," she said, acknowledging the bioengineer.

"Morning," he replied, though his tone carried a subtle tension. Everyone felt it, though none wanted to name it.

Anya slipped into the exercise harness and strapped her legs into the resistance units. Today's program was routine: squats, pulls, presses. Every repetition measured, every angle of motion recorded. Nothing unusual—except for the way her body responded.

The pull was lighter than expected. Her bones resisted less. Her muscles activated differently. The data confirmed it: adaptation was accelerating faster than anticipated.

"Anya?" Ezra's voice broke her concentration. "Your lower limb resistance is showing unexpected deviation."

She glanced at the monitor. The readout blinked a series of numbers she knew intimately: femur density, tibia alignment, quadricep strength. All were within expected Mars adaptation norms.

Yet... not really.

"The body is learning," she said quietly, almost to herself. "Learning too well."

Ezra's brow furrowed. "You mean... it's... adapting faster than it should?"

"Yes," she said. The word hung in the lab, heavy, tangible. "At this rate, Earth gravity would feel... hostile."

They both considered that. Humans had come to Mars expecting hardship, but not irreversibility. Not a physiological reshaping that would make returning to Earth an impossibility.

The next hours unfolded in repetitive, almost ceremonial precision. Anya moved through squats, presses, and cycles, monitoring heart rate, oxygen consumption, and muscle engagement. Every minute was logged. Every anomaly documented.

And yet, each repetition carried a growing sense of dread. Her body was betraying her in small increments. Flexibility in her joints increased unnaturally; bones that should have resisted stress seemed almost fragile in their new strength. Adaptation was elegance, efficiency—but it was also a silent erasure.

During the break, Anya stepped toward the observation viewport. Dust swirled lazily in the low light of the Martian afternoon. The colony hummed beneath her feet, silent and steady. She placed a hand on the reinforced glass, feeling its cool, unyielding surface. Outside, the landscape stretched endlessly, unchanging. And inside, the humans were changing.

Ezra approached, holding a tablet. "Check this," he said. Data scrolled across the screen: projected bone density and muscle composition over the next five sols. At the projected rate, no human returning to Earth would survive the first week. Even minimal gravity would crush them.

Anya swallowed, feeling the weight settle in her chest. "We're not just adapting," she whispered. "We're rewriting ourselves."

Ezra's expression was pale. "Not gradually," he said. "Not over centuries. Months. Sols. Weeks."

The day continued with procedural exercises, repeated measurements, and careful calibrations. Each action, each click of a button, each adjustment of a resistance band reminded her of the inevitability building quietly in the background.

She ran the treadmill simulation, noting how every step required less effort. Her stride lengthened slightly. The gravity-adjusted weights were lighter, yet she felt strain building in different places—small, unfamiliar tensions. Adaptation was rewriting not just capability, but expectation, intuition, memory.

By mid-afternoon, she realized she could no longer remember exactly how Earth felt beneath her feet. The pressure of two Gs. The subtle feedback of muscles and bones correcting in milliseconds. Only an abstract, imagined sensation remained, a phantom memory.

She closed her eyes, trying to recall jogging through the park as a child. The memory was sharp at first—grass underfoot, wind in her hair—but faded quickly. The muscles didn't remember. Her lungs didn't remember. Her bones didn't remember.

She opened her eyes. The treadmill data showed perfect alignment, perfect adaptation. Humans on Mars were evolving—or at least, reshaping themselves—in ways no one had fully anticipated.

Ezra cleared his throat. "We should report this," he said quietly. "The adaptation curve... it's beyond expected projections."

Anya shook her head. "It's within the limits of survival. Mars doesn't break us. It changes us. That's all."

They didn't need to say it aloud, but the unspoken truth was heavier than any report: Earth would not welcome them back. Not as they were. Returning wasn't merely dangerous—it would be impossible.

Later, Anya performed the final set of exercises, sweat dampening her brow. She logged every metric, double-checked the readings, and recorded her observations with meticulous care. Habit. Procedure. Routine. The work was comforting. It anchored her to something that still made sense.

But the physiological truth was undeniable. The human body on Mars was not temporary; it was permanent.

She returned to her quarters as the artificial evening settled over the habitat. Dust drifted along the corridors in faint, suspended streams, reflecting the dim light. She sat at her workstation, staring at the data. Every graph, every table, every metric confirmed what she already knew: the colony was thriving, perfectly, and yet humans were no longer entirely human in the way they had left Earth.

A soft chime from the monitoring console reminded her of the small personal touch in all of this. She had set reminders for hydration, rest, and minor exercise intervals. Mars demanded compliance. And she complied, because that was survival too.

Anya thought of the first children born on Mars, of the infants whose bones would grow accustomed to this gravity from birth. For them, Earth would be a legend, a story, a foreign, cruel memory. The colony would flourish—but the species would be altered irreversibly.

She exhaled, letting herself feel the tension in her chest relax slightly. Tomorrow, the exercises would repeat. Measurements would continue. Adaptation would progress. Routine would hold them together even as their bodies silently diverged from the past.

And in that quiet, relentless, unobserved transformation, Anya felt both awe and unease. Mars didn't need to destroy them. It only needed to exist—and the humans would change themselves.

Before sleep, she glanced once more at the viewport. Dust swirled endlessly in the fading light, indifferent, eternal. Her reflection stared back at her, leaner, taller, subtly altered. She wondered if tomorrow, or the day after, she would recognize herself at all.

And somewhere, beyond reach, Earth waited.

But Mars didn't care.

And that, Anya realized, was the most terrifying part.

## Sunrise delay

Elara Mendez sat cross-legged on the observation deck floor, helmet off, visor tucked beside her. The lights of the habitat had dimmed to simulate dawn, but she didn't need the artificial sun to know when morning was coming. She had learned the rhythms of Mars: the subtle heating of the panels, the way dust lifted from the northern ridges, the gentle hum of the colony's systems like a slow, omnipresent heartbeat.

Outside, the red horizon stretched endlessly, vast and patient. She leaned forward, pressing her palms to the cool surface of the viewport. The texture was smooth, but it felt like a boundary between worlds: the warmth of human life pressed against the indifferent eternity of the planet.

Elara had been awake for hours, waiting. Not for anything specific, not for a message, not for a storm—but for the sunrise. Mars' sun was faint, distant, almost timid, and she wanted to see it crest the horizon in person, uninterrupted by artificial lights or schedules.

"Why here?" came a voice softly behind her.

She didn't turn immediately. When she did, it was only a fraction of a turn—enough to see Jonas, standing awkwardly with his mug of rehydrated coffee. His hair stuck up at odd angles, and a smudge of dust clung to his sleeve.

"Why what?" she asked.

"This. Sitting. Waiting."

Elara smiled faintly, though her eyes remained on the horizon. "Because the sunrise here... it's different. You have to earn it. You have to be still enough to notice it."

Jonas approached slowly, sitting beside her. They didn't touch; space was generous here, even inside the habitat.

"I've seen a hundred sunrises," he said. "On Earth."

"And they were bright and loud," Elara said. "Here... here it's quiet. Patient. It doesn't announce itself. You find it in fragments. Dust lifting, light bending across a ridge, color changing imperceptibly for hours until suddenly—bam. There it is."

He chuckled softly, not to mock, but because her words painted a picture he could almost feel. He shifted slightly, leaning against the wall beside her, and for a moment, neither of them spoke.

The first faint edge of orange appeared along the distant horizon. Not dramatic. Not bold. A whisper of warmth.

Elara's breath caught. She didn't move. Her eyes traced the slow curve of light creeping upward. It was as if Mars itself was revealing a secret, a quiet wonder reserved for those patient enough to wait.

Jonas watched her face instead of the horizon. The way her lips parted slightly, the faint tremor in her hand resting on the glass, the way her eyes seemed to glow as they reflected the growing light.

"It's... beautiful," he said, almost in disbelief. "I didn't think I could feel this way here. Not after months."

Elara turned to him, and for the first time, their eyes met fully. She saw the awe mirrored in his expression, and the tiny threads of human connection pulled taut between them. A smile curved her lips.

"You never know what Mars will give you," she whispered. "You think it's barren, indifferent. But if you stop, if you actually stop, it rewards you. Quietly, endlessly."

The light grew, faint shadows appearing on the interior of the deck as if the planet itself were spilling onto them. Dust motes danced in the beams like suspended stars. Every particle glittered, refracted, became a small universe in miniature.

Jonas extended a hand. Hesitantly. Elara took it. Not a romantic gesture, not exactly. Something simpler, human, grounding. Connection in a place where connection was scarce.

They sat together, watching, breathing, waiting. The sun rose higher, slowly, deliberately. Time lost its rigidity. Minutes could have been hours; hours could have been seconds. It didn't matter. The planet dictated its own rhythm, and they yielded to it.

Elara pointed to a ridge far to the south. "See that curve of rock? Watch the light there."

The ridge glowed faintly, gold where it had been rust. Shadows shifted slowly, impossibly, and the two of them were silent witnesses to something profoundly alive. Not alive in the way humans understood life, but alive in presence, in immensity, in patient, deliberate existence.

Jonas whispered, "I wish I could freeze this. Live here forever in this moment."

Elara squeezed his hand gently. "You can. You just have to notice it. That's all Mars asks of you. To be present. To see."

A small alarm chimed from the control console nearby, signaling routine diagnostics. They ignored it. For once, there was nothing more important than watching.

Hours passed—or maybe minutes. The simulated habitat sun continued its own cycle, but outside, the horizon painted a story of time that wasn't theirs to own. The warmth of the sun touched their faces through the viewport. Mars was patient, indifferent, vast. And yet, for those who stopped, it gave them the impossible: wonder.

Elara traced the outline of a dust cloud rising from a distant crater. "Look at that. No one told you to notice it. It's just... there."

Jonas leaned closer. "I see it. I see all of it."

They didn't speak again for a long time. Words would have spoiled it. Conversation was human; Mars required silence. Patience. Observation. Presence.

Finally, Elara rose, stretching. She turned to Jonas. "Come with me. To the northern ridge. The light will be perfect there tomorrow. You'll want to see it. I promise."

He nodded, quietly, but his eyes lingered on the horizon a moment longer. He didn't need to say it—he understood. This was the gift Mars offered to those who could stop and simply look.

And in that gift, in the shared awe, in the quiet holding of time, both of them felt something extraordinary. Hope. Connection. Wonder. The kind that made all the isolation, all the dust, all the relentless routine of Mars worthwhile.

Elara turned back to the window one last time before leaving. The sun had fully risen, spilling light across the red horizon. Dust motes sparkled in the golden glow. Shadows receded. And for a fleeting instant, she felt that the universe itself had paused—just for them—to show them what it meant to exist quietly, beautifully, and completely.

As they walked back to the living quarters, hands brushing, hearts quietly synchronized to the rhythm of the planet, Elara knew this would be a memory they carried forever. A moment when Mars, in its patience, had whispered something profound: life is not just survival. Life is noticing.

And in that moment, they both thought, without speaking, "I wish this could happen every day."

## First light on the last horizon

Addison Morgan crouched near the hydroponic garden, fingertips brushing over the delicate green shoots of Martian-grown lettuce. The light spilling through the viewport was pale, filtered through layers of dust and glass, but it was enough—enough for life, enough for hope. The plants shimmered faintly under the weak sun, each leaf a fragile defiance against a planet that demanded nothing, gave nothing, but allowed persistence.

The children stirred in the dormitories above. Their voices rose slowly at first, a soft chorus of yawns, giggles, and whispered excitement. Addison listened, heart tightening. Mars-born laughter had a different timbre, high and airy, shaped by gravity that was lighter than anything Earth had offered, shaped by lungs that inhaled thinner air and processed it efficiently. It was laughter stripped of Earthly cadence, yet pure, alive, unselfconscious.

Addison smiled, but the smile was tinged with melancholy. These were the first children born on Mars—the first generation who would never feel soil beneath their feet, who had never breathed the wind of another world, who knew Earth only as story and myth. And Earth... Earth had gone silent.

"Addy!"

The voice was small, insistent. A girl named Isha appeared at the edge of the garden, her brown eyes shining with curiosity. She clutched a slim, tablet-like device in her hands, the screen glowing faintly in the soft red light of the habitat.

"What is it, Isha?" Addison asked, standing carefully, bending only slightly to meet her height.

"I figured it out!" she said, her voice rising in excitement. "I know where Earth is!"

Addison's chest tightened, a mixture of pride and unease curling inside them. "Where?"

Isha pointed to the star charts on the device. "It's... somewhere over there," she said, gesturing vaguely toward the Martian sky beyond the viewport. "But it's gone quiet. I don't hear anything from it!"

Addison felt that familiar pang—the soft twist of dread that never fully left the colony. Children asked questions adults were never prepared for, questions so simple and innocent they fractured long-held illusions.

"Yes," Addison said softly, kneeling to her level. "Earth... is silent. And maybe it will stay that way."

Isha's brow furrowed. "But... is it still our home?"

Addison considered the question carefully, letting the silence stretch between them. Outside, dust swirled in faint spirals, drifting lazily across the plains like something half-alive. The hydroponic system hissed quietly as nutrient solution circulated through pipes, droplets catching the soft light like tiny stars. The rhythm was subtle, grounding, reminding Addison of the persistence of life in a world that offered no guidance, no audience, no reward beyond mere survival.

"Home," Addison said finally, "is what we make of it here. We grow it, we care for it, we live it. Mars is our home now."

Isha's eyes flickered between understanding and uncertainty. Children were adaptable, resilient, able to inhabit worlds adults could only simulate. Addison knew that her explanation would settle somewhere in Isha's mind, bending and twisting to fit her own perception of what "home" meant.

The rest of the children had begun gathering near the observation deck. Addison guided them, their small bodies moving with a grace born of low gravity. Hands reached to trace the viewport, noses pressed against glass, eyes wide at the endless red horizon beyond. Dust swirled in gentle eddies, sculpted by invisible winds. Distant ridges glimmered, mountains blurred in faint atmospheric haze, and the sun rose weakly, indifferent to their presence.

One boy, older than the others, whispered, "It's... beautiful."

"Yes," Addison said. "And it's ours. We are alive here. We can be anything here. We can watch the sun rise every day if we want. We can learn everything Mars can teach us."

Isha tilted her head, hesitating, eyes wide. "Even... stories about Earth?"

Addison smiled faintly. "Even stories," they said, voice soft. "But Earth is a memory now. A guide, perhaps. Not a place we can visit anymore."

The children nodded, some exchanging quiet glances. Mars did not rush. Mars did not demand. Its indifference was a teacher in itself, showing patience, observation, and resilience. The vast emptiness beyond the viewport whispered lessons older than human memory, lessons about attention, survival, and the beauty of persistence.

Addison watched as the children began inventing words for what they saw: a swirling dust devil became curlwind, sunlight filtering through fine red particles became glintfall, and the faint hum of the habitat's systems was whisperpulse. Each word was precise, born from need, from observation, from the necessity of naming something so new, so unlike anything their parents had known.

Addison took a deep breath. The weight of history pressed down—the children's adaptation, the colony's survival, the fading memory of Earth. Bones had hardened differently here, minds had stretched, and memory had become selective. The pulse of Mars claimed them in subtle, inexorable increments. Yet in the same breath, Addison felt awe, hope, and quiet triumph.

"Come," Addison said, gesturing toward a ridge visible through the deck's glass. "Let's explore. Let's notice. Let's remember how to see this world, truly see it."

The children followed, stepping lightly, balancing with ease in gravity that was always slightly too weak, always slightly too strange. They moved like dancers, explorers, inventors of movement itself. Addison followed, feeling the strain of old muscles, the weight of Earth-conditioned expectations, and the exhilaration of watching a generation that knew no other life.

They stopped together at the highest viewport. The Martian horizon stretched endlessly. Dust swirled in fine lines, sunlight glimmered faintly on ridges, and somewhere, beyond visible range, mountains waited, eternal and indifferent. The children pressed their hands to the glass, tracing shapes, pointing, inventing words, laughing softly at discoveries no adult had imagined.

Addison knelt beside Isha again. "Do you understand now?" they asked. "Home is not where Earth once was. Home is here. It is what we grow. What we care for. What we notice."

Isha nodded, small hand slipping into Addison's. Warm. Real. Present. In that touch, Addison felt the impossible: life, even in the absence of Earth, could flourish, intimately, beautifully, against all odds.

"Let's go," Addison said, voice low but steady. "We have work to do. We grow food. We learn. We explore. And we watch. Always watch."

The children scattered slightly, still holding hands in pairs, calling invented words for shapes in the dust, for light patterns, for wind currents. Their laughter echoed softly against the walls, mingling with the subtle hum of life-support systems. Outside, the wind sculpted the Martian plains with quiet precision. The planet did not notice. Did not care.

And yet, in that indifference, humans found meaning. Connection. Wonder. Life.

Addison lingered a moment longer at the deck, watching the children move, listening to their laughter, inhaling the faint scent of the nutrient-rich hydroponics air. The sun climbed higher, pale and fragile, spilling light over every ridge, every dust mote, every small human heart beating against the vast, patient, indifferent world.

Mars had not needed to destroy them. It had only needed to exist.

And in its existence, in that eternal, indifferent presence, humans had learned the most extraordinary truth: life, attention, connection—small, fragile, human things—were enough.

They would grow. They would watch. They would invent, discover, and remember, even if Earth no longer did.

Addison turned one last time to the horizon, breathing in the filtered light, letting the quiet swell of awe and hope fill them. This first light—the sunrise on the last horizon—would remain in memory, etched into the children's minds, into the colony's rhythms, into humanity itself.

Here, on Mars, home was not inherited. Home was made. And for the first generation, it was already theirs

## Observing the void

Nina Salvetti arrived at the comms bay long before the habitat's artificial sunrise. The narrow corridor hummed beneath her boots with the steady pulse of life support systems, the filtered hum of fans and pumps weaving an inaudible rhythm that felt almost alive. The walls of the bay glowed faintly from soft amber overhead lights, casting long, angular shadows across consoles and cabling. In the dimness, the silence pressed in—not a void, not emptiness, but a weight, patient and deliberate.

She moved slowly, methodically. Boots clicking on the grated floor, fingers brushing lightly along the edges of consoles, adjusting overhead lights to a softer glow. These were small gestures, habitual, almost ceremonial. Each day, before anything else, she arrived early to witness the first moments of her post—alone, in quiet, surrounded by the steady heartbeat of systems that never slept.

She sat at her station, activating the array of monitors that traced the invisible web of communication between Mars and the world it had left behind. Normally, the screens would flicker with activity: automated pings, telemetry, faint bursts of chatter from deep-space relay stations, minor anomalies, and the occasional crackle of an Earth-born transmission. These signals were always faint, distant—but they existed. Today, they did not.

Not absent entirely. The systems hummed, alive, counting, tracking, logging. But the vital noise—the heartbeat of Earth—was gone.

Nina ran her hands over the keyboard, hesitating, as though touching the keys could stir the signals to life. Amplify, reroute, override—her fingers hovered, conscious of the weight of choice. A single command could broadcast the anomaly, could flag it, could summon analysis, procedure, consequence. But something rooted her to the chair, made her pause. The silence was not accidental. Not a technical glitch or a temporary lapse. It was deliberate, patient, full of implication.

She pulled up the historical logs. They stretched back decades, tracing faint pulses, patterns, decays of signal, distortions, and errors. Years of information had been recorded, logged, filed away. Every shift, every ping, every minor system anomaly was documented, etched into electronic memory. Then... nothing. Not a glitch. Not a misfire. A hollow, patternless void that pressed into her mind with increasing intensity.

Her own heartbeat, loud in the quiet, became a metronome for reflection.

"Morning, Nina," came a voice behind her, soft, calm, almost casual. Damien, her shift supervisor, leaned against the doorway. His posture was easy, trained to look confident, but the shadow in his eyes mirrored the unease she felt.

"You've seen it too?" Nina asked, not turning.

He nodded. "It's... consistent. Entirely quiet. No interference. No signals. It's as if Earth... stopped trying."

She scrolled through the logs again, carefully tracing timestamps, cross-referencing satellite relays, recalculating expected signals against actual arrivals. Every ping had vanished. Every routine message had stopped. Not failed. Not delayed. Simply—ceased.

"I can report this," she said. "Raise a flag, generate alerts, follow protocol."

Damien shook his head. "Why? What will it change? Maybe Earth still exists. Maybe not. But what difference does it make if we... act?"

The moral weight of his words pressed down. Years of conditioning, drilled responses for crises, for measurable danger, for catastrophe—none of it applied here. This absence demanded a choice that was not procedural, not quantifiable. It demanded a judgment: action, or non-action. Both carried consequences, both ethical, invisible, inexorably binding.

Nina's fingers hovered over the console. Report. Ignore. Both were deliberate, both irreversible in subtle ways. To act might accomplish nothing. To ignore might render her complicit in an erasure that was already underway.

Hours passed. She monitored, logged, cross-checked. Every routine signal check confirmed the same haunting anomaly: silence.

The comms bay was alive with equipment, yet each hum of a fan, each pulse of a relay, each soft click of a console key felt magnified in the absence of external noise. She noticed the fine vibration of power conduits beneath her feet, the way fluorescent indicators pulsed rhythmically, as though the habitat itself were breathing. And in that mechanical heartbeat, the absence of Earth was sharp, palpable.

Midmorning, Nina rose and moved to the viewport. The red plains stretched endlessly, dust rising in slow spirals sculpted by invisible Martian winds. Light from the weak sun played across ridges and valleys, soft and indifferent. The colony thrived beneath her, humming quietly, a miniature ecosystem of people, plants, machines. Routine continued as always. Mars did not care. The absence outside her screens—the lack of an audience, a home planet to witness, guide, or warn—suddenly seemed almost natural.

Damien approached, slow, deliberate. "Do we... tell anyone?"

Nina shook her head. She realized the answer had settled in her mind hours ago. Reporting would produce nothing. Routine demanded acknowledgment, but survival demanded adaptation, patience, and quiet continuation. Survival here was not measured in alarms or heroics. Survival was invisible, persistent, uninterrupted.

Returning to her station, she began systematically deleting the anomalous logs. Every file overwritten. Every timestamp adjusted. Every trace of the silence erased. Her hands moved with mechanical precision, fingers steady, guided by instinct, routine, and a strange sense of necessity.

As she worked, her mind wandered, quietly, toward philosophical reflections she rarely allowed herself. Silence, she realized, was not absence. It was intention, patience, presence. It shaped cognition, moral reflection, and identity. A home that stopped speaking, a world that refused its signals, demanded participation, demanded consent. To ignore it, to erase it, was to acknowledge the supremacy of Mars' indifference over Earthly memory.

Hours blurred. Monitoring screens reflected the artificial sun climbing overhead, casting faint orange illumination across the room. Dust motes floated lazily in shafts of light, moving according to gravity and air currents, oblivious to human concern. Nina continued her work, each deletion a meditation on power, responsibility, and survival.

By late afternoon, she paused. Damien leaned against a console, silent, watching, perhaps weighing the moral gravity alongside her.

"Do we ever wonder," he said finally, "if this is worse than a disaster?"

Nina met his gaze. "Yes," she admitted softly. "Every sol. Because there is no emergency here. There is no panic. There is only quiet. And quiet... teaches differently."

They stood together in companionable silence, listening to the hum of machinery, the soft pulse of the habitat, the faint whisper of dust against glass. Mars offered no instruction, no judgment. It simply existed.

When evening arrived, the habitat dimmed its lights to simulate sunset. Nina lingered at the viewport, watching dust swirl and settle, illuminated by the soft artificial glow. Earth's signals were absent, erased, or silent. No alarms rang. No consequences emerged. The colony persisted. Humans moved, learned, slept, ate, laughed quietly in routines that were flawless, unbroken, uninterrupted.

Damien came by one last time. "All clear?"

"Yes," Nina said softly, and for the first time, allowed herself a trace of a smile. But her eyes betrayed the unease she carried, the moral compromise of perfection. They had chosen to ignore the silence, to erase the evidence, to participate willingly in the quiet erasure of a home they could not return to.

Silence, she realized, was a presence. Patient. Deliberate. Infinite. And within that presence, humans could continue. Routine, life, survival—yes—but never fully human in the messy, unpredictable way that the old Earth demanded.

Mars had no alarms. It required no catastrophes. It needed only observers—humans who could continue, who could monitor, who could log, who could erase, who could exist.

Nina logged out as the sol ended, her shift complete. She lingered one last moment at the viewport. Dust glimmered faintly in the weak light. It was beautiful, patient, indifferent. She had erased the silence, but she could not erase its lesson.

Earth was gone—or silent. The colony persisted. And the quiet... would remain.

It would shape the humans within it, day after day, sol after sol, until silence itself became routine, until absence became instruction, until quiet became existence.

And Nina understood, fully, that this was survival. Not heroics. Not contact. Not triumph. But survival all the same—and it was enough.

## The last Earth joke

Soren Callas arrived at the auditorium well before the day officially began. The artificial sunrise had not yet touched the interior panels, leaving the space dim, quiet, and waiting. He ran a hand along the steel wall as he walked, the coolness grounding him, reminding him of the habitat's resilience, the discipline of construction, the isolation of a world that didn't notice. Outside, the Martian wind swept across distant ridges, sending subtle tremors through the habitat's frame. The hum of the ventilation systems and life-support pumps created a gentle pulse, steady, low, a heartbeat for a place that needed no heart but had found one in human persistence.

He checked the projector first, running through every cable, every lens, ensuring the lights would shine evenly across the stage. The seats, bolted firmly to the floor, gleamed faintly in the overhead dimness. Dust-resistant panels and reinforced walls made the space sterile, almost brutalist, but functional. Nothing here was decorative; everything had a purpose. Mars had no interest in theater or performance, and yet Soren's world depended on it.

Flipping through the deck of slides, Soren examined the jokes, anecdotes, and punchlines compiled over decades. Earth humor. Earth rhythm. Earth timing. He rehearsed under his breath, quietly, softly:

"What do you call a Martian who tells a lie?..."

He stopped, shaking his head. Too familiar. Too obvious. Too heavy with Earth's memory. Too old. Here, on Mars, humor had to breathe differently, move differently, survive differently.

The doors slid open. A hush preceded the children, small shadows moving into the seats, some bouncing slightly on the tips of their shoes in anticipation. Their laughter, light and airy, carried a cadence shaped by low gravity, thin air, and a world entirely unlike the one from which Earth's humor had sprung.

"Morning, Soren!" a small voice chirped. The children clustered around the edges of the auditorium, restless, curious, eyes wide as they scanned the stage, the projector, the lights, the very walls of the habitat.

He smiled faintly. "Good morning," he said. "Find your seats, and we'll begin. Today, we'll try something new."

He clicked the first slide. The classic Earth joke appeared, bright and familiar against the steel background:

"Why did the chicken cross the road?"

A few of the older children attempted polite smiles, fleeting traces of recognition in muscles that had never felt sidewalks, never crossed streets, never experienced traffic, never engaged with a world that existed beyond red dust and habitat walls. Others stared, blank, as though the concept itself were abstract.

Soren swallowed. He had expected resistance. He had not expected silence so thick it seemed to absorb sound. The punchline—"To get to the other side"—was a stone dropped into a vacuum. It landed, yes, but there was no echo, no resonance, no acknowledgment.

He took a breath and swiped the next slide. A small observational quip about Mars itself appeared: dust, routine, humidity, airlocks.

"What did the dust say to the vent?"

The children looked at one another, puzzled. One giggled faintly. A tiny sound, hesitant, like the first raindrop on dry soil.

"...Nothing. It was already inside."

The laughter spread slowly, tentative at first, then louder, more confident, catching rhythm and volume in small increments. Timing, absurdity, the ridiculous resonance—they understood it. They connected with it. They adapted it. Mars had shaped them. Their humor reflected it.

Soren felt a pang in his chest. Earth's humor, once so familiar, so foundational, had failed. It no longer resonated. But here, a new rhythm had emerged, drawn from dust, routines, shared struggle, and the subtle absurdities of a red planet indifferent to human presence.

He continued. Improvisation followed improvisation: the hiss of airlocks, the squelch of recycled water, the hum of habitat life-support. Each punchline tested lightly, observed, adjusted. The children responded, experimenting with gestures, mimicking intonation, inventing their own punchlines.

He paused mid-set, letting them mimic a gag about oxygen recirculation. One child, barely seven, whispered to another:

"Do you think Earth even had good jokes?"

The older child shrugged, eyes wide. "Maybe. But I like ours better."

Soren swallowed again. The truth pressed against him: this was not loss. This was evolution. Culture, humor, shared joy—it had adapted. Earth was memory. Mars was the present. The colony's shared reality had shifted, quietly, irreversibly.

The afternoon stretched. Slides, punchlines, improvisations flowed together in a rhythm unique to the sol. The children laughed, argued, shared timing cues, experimented with narrative arcs. Soren followed them, adjusting, responding, guiding, laughing quietly under his breath.

"What's heavier: a ton of regolith or a ton of air?" he asked.

The children debated, shouted guesses, corrected one another, laughed at mistakes, delighted in discovery. No punchline landed as a line. The punchline was presence itself—the participation, the absurdity, the adaptation.

He watched as a small circle formed among them, inventing their own sketches, mimicking the hiss of airlocks, the swish of dust through vents, the patter of recycled water. Each microcosm of humor became a laboratory of Mars-born expression, playful, precise, self-contained, alive.

Soren moved quietly among them, listening, guiding, observing. The audience had transformed into creators. The performance was no longer his alone; it belonged to the children, to the sol, to the habitat itself.

Evening arrived, and the artificial lights dimmed, simulating a sunset that had never touched Mars. The children filed out slowly, still giggling, whispering, humming improvised punchlines, practicing gestures, inventing words for dust patterns, and subtle quirks of the habitat.

Soren remained, alone on the stage. He ran a hand over the smooth steel, feeling the vibrations of distant dust storms through the walls, listening to the faint hum of the life-support system, noticing the way the air moved, how the ventilation hissed with precise, indifferent rhythm.

He thought of Earth—its streets, its roads, its crowded laughter, its libraries of jokes, its culture preserved in ink and memory. It was obsolete here. Yet something deeper had arisen. Something richer. Something human, entirely adapted to the slow, indifferent rhythms of Mars.

He whispered softly to the empty auditorium, a vow, a prayer, a recognition:

"Let them laugh. Let them remember who they are—here, now."

And for the first time that sol, in the quiet hum and the red dust-light spilling faintly across the floor, Soren laughed. Not at Earth, not at Mars, not at himself. At life itself. Fragile, absurd, extraordinary, human life.

Outside, dust swirled like tiny comets. The planet neither smiled nor fumed, neither noticed nor cared. But the humans did.

Here, culture was not stolen. It was transformed. It was alive.

## Bones in the wild

Dr. Liora Venn adjusted the straps on the exoskeletal harness, the soft clicks and micro-hisses of the locking mechanisms filling the quiet lab. The Martian sunlight filtered through the high dome windows, casting long, dusty shadows across the floor. Outside, wind swirled across the plains, tracing invisible lines over ridges and craters, carrying fine particles in slow, endless spirals. The colony hummed softly beneath her feet, its systems alive, precise, and indifferent.

She glanced at the monitors. Heart rates, oxygen saturation, muscle tension, bone density—all readings within expected parameters for human physiology on Mars. The colony's algorithms predicted every heartbeat, every breath, every movement. And yet, Liora felt the pull of anticipation: one anomaly, one deviation, could rewrite her understanding of life in low gravity.

Today, she was observing the children—Martian-born humans, the first to live their entire lives without Earth's pull. They moved differently, subtly, almost imperceptibly. Their limbs elongated slightly; their steps arced higher; their bones retained flexibility her Earth-trained eyes could scarcely quantify. They were strong, not in the violent way of soldiers or athletes, but in resilience, in adaptability, in the quiet mastery of their environment.

"Ready, Jaren?" she asked, as the boy stepped onto the platform. The exoskeletal sensors clicked into place around his small frame.

Jaren, twelve years old, grinned. "Always!"

She nodded and began the session, calibrating the harness to record gait, stride, and impact force. Each jump, each spin, each crouch against Mars' one-third gravity revealed small adjustments. Muscles fired differently; balance shifted; reactions slowed and then corrected in milliseconds. The colony had predicted most of this, yes. But watching it live—the subtle elegance of adaptation—was impossible to simulate.

Across the room, other children played with low-gravity balls, using their elongated leaps to send spheres soaring higher than Earth physics would allow. Liora recorded, measured, logged. Everything precise. Everything expected. Yet even as she noted the readings, she felt a faint, gnawing unease: these children were not human in the way she remembered. Not fully. And yet... they were more human than she had ever seen, if humanity was defined by resilience, curiosity, and improvisation.

Hours passed. She rotated through tests: balance beams, jump arcs, strength calibration. Each movement a study in evolution without ceremony. Liora scribbled notes furiously, noting the divergence from Earth norms. The children did not complain; they thrived. Their laughter—light, unfiltered, sometimes explosive—filled the lab, bouncing softly against the steel walls.

She paused to watch a pair of girls spinning through the air, twisting and landing with a grace that defied calculation. "Your bones are learning to love this place," she murmured. "And I... I am learning to understand you."

The midday sun climbed higher, and she took a rare break, sitting by the viewport. Dust devils rose lazily across the ridges, spinning and dissolving without fanfare. She traced their arcs in her mind, noting the parallel with her own observations: both human and planetary adaptation occurring independently, silently, perfectly.

A soft alarm pinged from the console. One of the younger children, barely eight, had stumbled during a jump. Liora rushed over, gently checking the small body. Pulse steady. No injury beyond bruised pride. She adjusted the harness, reset the calibration, and helped the child regain balance.

It was a reminder: Mars did not protect them. Mars did not intervene. Every stumble, every misstep, every small failure was human alone, mediated by the colony's systems, the tools they had built, and the patient guidance of adults. The planet remained indifferent, the children thrived, and Liora noted the quiet lessons: resilience, adaptation, observation.

By afternoon, she began her final measurements, observing a group of children practicing climbing on a low-gravity recreation wall. Muscles, tendons, joints all adapted subtly to the demands of their environment. Bones flexed differently. Tendons stretched more easily. Movements appeared almost balletic in their fluidity. Each child was a small, living experiment, unconsciously rewriting the blueprint of humanity.

Liora's mind wandered as she recorded the readings. She thought of Earth, the gravity her own body remembered, the history of evolution under its pull. Here, the rules had changed. Survival was no longer an act of struggle against danger but a continuous negotiation with indifference. Life did not need heroics. Life did not need fear. Life simply persisted.

She scribbled in her log: "Musculoskeletal adaptation proceeding at predicted rates. Psychomotor development enhanced in low gravity. Children exhibit high problem-solving capability under environmental constraints. Observed laughter and play suggest robust emotional health. Humanity is diverging. Will continue to monitor."

Even as she wrote, she felt a weight pressing softly at the edges of her awareness. Divergence was not merely physical. Mars was rewriting the human experience in subtle, imperceptible ways: the way they moved, the way they learned, the way they remembered. Memory of Earth, of gravity, of struggle—already fading.

Late afternoon arrived. She allowed the children free time. Some skated along magnetic floors, using handrails to push and spin. Others jumped in arcs, learning the limits of their own bodies. Liora observed quietly, fascinated and a little unsettled. She realized that the children did not need the simulations she had painstakingly prepared—they invented their own. Rules emerged organically, shaped by necessity and curiosity, not instruction.

"Dr. Venn," one child called out, pointing to the viewport. A faint dust devil twisted across the horizon, a miniature tornado of red particles. "Look! It's playing!"

She smiled. "Yes. It is... exactly what it is."

The child tilted their head. "It's like it's alive!"

"Not alive," Liora corrected softly, "but patient. It doesn't need to notice us. It exists regardless. And we... we learn from it."

Evening crept in. The light softened, long shadows stretching across the lab. Children gathered to unwind, sharing observations about the day. Jaren showed her a new jump he had perfected. A small, triumphant demonstration. Liora felt a twinge of pride, tinged with melancholy: she was witnessing the first generation of humans not shaped by Earth's conditions, not bounded by its gravity, not tethered to its culture.

She prepared the final log entry for the sol:

"Observations complete. No anomalies beyond expected adaptation. Humans thriving, diverging from Earth norms. Physical, cognitive, emotional development proceeding. Mars indifferent. Life adapts. Humanity persists. The first generation of Martian-born humans does not require the hazards that defined their ancestors' survival. They define new rules. We record, observe, and bear witness. The planet watches, silent, eternal."

Liora stepped to the viewport once more, letting her gaze drift across the undulating plains. Dust devils spun lazily, ridges glowed faintly under the weak sun, the sky muted but infinite. The children's laughter echoed softly behind her.

She exhaled, softly, letting the pulse of the colony, the heartbeat of the children, and the patient rotation of Mars fill her senses. Life here was fragile, delicate, but unassailable. Humanity was becoming something new.

Bones in the wind. Limbs adapted, minds expanded, laughter evolved. Humanity endured—different, transformed—but undeniably alive.

## The Quietist betrayal

Elior Vance arrived at the maintenance bay before the artificial sunrise, as usual. The hum of the habitat was low and steady, a pulse beneath his feet that felt almost comforting. Rows of consoles glowed softly, their lights calibrated to mimic the early dawn. For a moment, he paused, letting his eyes wander over the smooth steel panels, the neatly coiled cables, the ordered trays of diagnostic tools. Everything was in its place. Everything worked. Everything obeyed him—or so it seemed.

"Morning, Elior," Selene's voice cut through the quiet. She leaned casually against the far console, arms crossed, a faint smirk tugging at her lips. Her hair fell in a careless arc over one shoulder, and her gaze lingered on the terminal she had been "adjusting."

Elior forced a polite smile. "Morning. Routine day, I assume?"

"Routine for you. Adventure for me," she said lightly. Her eyes flicked toward a cluster of sensors at the far end of the bay—ones she didn't have authorization to manipulate. A pang of unease prickled at Elior, but he said nothing. Not yet.

The morning passed in quiet, meticulous work. Elior ran calibration sequences on the air circulation system, verified filtration rates, and logged every reading with the precision that had become instinct. He noticed the subtle changes Selene had made—tiny, almost imperceptible tweaks that bypassed minor safety checks. He could have reported them. He should have. But he didn't.

Instead, he recorded the deviations silently in his private log, noting their effects: marginal gains in efficiency, no immediate risk, and a faint moral dissonance that seemed to settle like dust in the pit of his stomach.

By midmorning, the first faint stirrings of tension had grown. Elior caught Selene rerouting a power circuit to accelerate an experiment in the biology lab. It was clever, almost elegant. But it was also unauthorized.

"Selene," he said quietly, approaching her. "That's not within protocol. You know I can report this."

She turned, expression calm, serene even. "I know. And I also know it won't fail. I've thought it through. Efficiency isn't crime, Elior. It's adaptation."

He wanted to argue, to insist that rules were not optional, that safety mattered, that even minor deviations carried consequences. But the words lodged in his throat. Her confidence, her ease—it had a way of bending the conversation, bending him. And he realized something unsettling: the choice to act or to ignore was now his alone.

By noon, Elior had shadowed her through three more minor breaches: bypassed sensor checks, small recalibrations of automated water recirculators, and the subtle acceleration of hydroponic nutrient cycles. None of them catastrophic. None of them dangerous. But each one pushed the boundaries of trust, routine, and ethics.

He found himself reasoning: The colony will not fail. No one will get hurt. It's better to allow this than to fracture human relationships over minutiae. It is... rational.

But rationality had never felt this hollow.

Lunch passed quietly. Elior ate mechanically, sipping nutrient paste from a small cup, eyes flicking to Selene every few minutes. She moved around the bay with fluid grace, unconcerned, humming softly under her breath as she adjusted systems that technically weren't hers to touch. Her laughter, faint and musical, was a thread of warmth in the sterile room—but it also gnawed at him. Every small act of mischief, every choice to circumvent protocol, highlighted the quiet moral compromises that underpinned their survival.

In the afternoon, the colony's children passed through the corridors, their low-gravity jumps echoing faintly against the steel walls. Martian-born humans, unburdened by Earth's memory, laughed at games Elior couldn't fully understand. He envied their innocence. He envied the simplicity with which they approached life. They had no need to reconcile ethics with survival; they had no need to reconcile loyalty with rules.

Selene approached him as he monitored the oxygen systems. "You're too tense," she said softly. "Relax. We keep everything alive. Isn't that enough?"

He shook his head. "Not... enough. Not for me."

Her eyes softened. "Then maybe it's time to stop trying to hold onto Earth."

Evening arrived slowly. Elior followed Selene to the engineering hub, where she prepared a more significant rerouting: diverting redundant power to the habitat's experimental incubator. He recognized it immediately—not dangerous, but undeniably wrong by the book.

He hesitated at the console. He could intervene. He could send an automated report. He could, with the press of a key, expose her, fracture the fragile trust they had built, call every system into question.

And yet... he didn't.

Instead, he adjusted a few minor parameters, masking the breach without undoing her work entirely. The incubator functioned, the experiment accelerated, the colony remained stable. No alarms rang. No errors appeared. And in the quiet that followed, Elior felt a weight settle across his chest.

It was not relief. Not pride. It was the awareness that he had made a decision he could not undo, a choice to allow compromise in the name of cohesion, survival, and human connection.

He returned to his personal console, logging the day:

"Minor ethical compromise observed. Decision made to allow adaptation and minor deviations to preserve human trust and colony cohesion. No immediate risk detected. Systems operational. Humans persist. Morality complicated. The sol ends."

The lights dimmed for the simulated sunset. Elior leaned against the viewport, tracing the muted red horizon. A small dust spiral traced across the plains, and children's laughter echoed faintly from the recreation module.

He realized that human life on Mars persisted not only through routines, skill, and science—but through quiet choices, compromises, and trust stretched thin across isolation. They were adapting, yes. They were surviving. But survival was not morality. Survival was not courage. Survival was the slow, persistent negotiation between fear, loyalty, and self-interest.

Selene passed by, smiling faintly. "You'll be fine," she said. "You'll see. We all adapt."

Elior nodded. Not because he agreed. Not because he had resolved the tension. But because silence, complicity, and human connection had won today. And tomorrow, the same quiet negotiation would begin again.

He exhaled, long and steady. The day was over, the sol closed. Humanity persisted. The colony thrived. And yet, he knew—the quietest betrayals, the invisible compromises, the moral shadows—would accumulate, shaping them in ways no log could record, no algorithm could anticipate.

Mars need not intervene. Humanity could fracture itself quietly, invisibly, even while everything seemed to work.

And Elior understood, finally, that this was one more lesson of survival: to endure is not always to be righteous. To live is not always to be whole.

The sol ended. Systems hummed. The humans thrived. And trust, fragile and invisible, settled over the habitat like a slow, persistent pulse, waiting for the next decision, the next compromise, the next choice that would define not survival, but the shape of their humanity.

## Archives of silence

Clementine Walker  arrived at the Cultural Archives before the artificial sunrise. The habitat's lights were dimmed, a faint, muted glow that brushed against the polished steel floors. She paused at the threshold, inhaling a breath she barely noticed she was holding, listening to the low hum of life-support systems vibrating softly beneath her boots. In this quiet hour, the entire colony seemed to hold its breath with her, waiting for her to start the day.

She approached the main console, fingers brushing lightly over the keyboard, and pulled up the logs from Earth. Hundreds of terabytes of transmissions, media clips, educational content, history lessons—all carefully cataloged over decades, meticulously preserved. And yet, the most recent entries were hollow. Static. Silence. Signals that should have ticked across the screens—faint voices, minor fluctuations in telemetry, even Earth's ordinary errors—were absent.

For years, Clementine had trained herself to treat gaps in data as anomalies, something to be corrected or investigated. But now, nothing had failed. No error codes, no system faults, no interference. The absence was deliberate—or so it felt to her. Each empty file, each missing transmission, carried a subtle weight that pressed at her chest.

"Morning, Clementine."

She flinched at the voice, turning to see Aric Vey, her colleague in the Cultural Department, leaning casually against a support pillar. His hair was mussed, his expression deliberately easy, though Clementine could see the tension beneath it. "Morning," she replied softly.

"You've seen it too," he said, gesturing at the floating screens that displayed the silent logs.

"Yes." She kept her gaze fixed on the data. "Every feed. Every relay. Empty. Nothing new. No errors. Just... nothing."

Aric nodded. "And no alarms. Everything still works. I guess that's... something." His voice faltered slightly at the end.

Clementine exhaled. "Something, yes. But it's not enough."

By mid-morning, the children began to drift into the Archives. Martian-born humans, some barely seven, some edging into their teenage years, moved through the rooms with a combination of curiosity and careful chaos. Gravity's soft pull made them float slightly with every step, hover for a second before touching down. Clementine had grown used to the quiet grace of their movements, the way they observed without fear, unconsciously testing the space, the air, the lighting, the books.

"Tell us again," a small voice chirped. It was Iona, barely seven, her hair cut in a blunt line across her forehead. She tugged gently at Mara's sleeve. "The story of Earth. The one with the... the river."

Clementine knelt, bringing herself to the child's level. "You mean the story of the Nile?"

Iona nodded eagerly. "Yes! And the people who lived near it, and the boats."

She began to recount the tale, her words bright and imaginative, and Clementine listened, biting her lip as familiar names and events twisted under the child's retelling. Boats that had never existed became flying vessels; kings became children; minor gods became mischievous animals. Every sentence added a flourish of creativity, but every detail was a deviation from fact.

"Close," Clementine said carefully, smoothing a strand of hair from Iona's face. "Not quite like that. The river was real, and the people were real, but..." She trailed off, realizing the futility. Their memory of Earth was not history—it was myth.

"Why does it matter?" Iona asked, wide-eyed. "If we make it up, isn't it better?"

Mara's chest tightened. She wanted to explain the importance of accuracy, of preservation, of connection to a past that had already begun to slip. And yet... the child had a point. The story lived, even if altered, and imagination made it survive in ways the archives never could.

By midday, Clementine had retreated to her workstation, a small cluster of terminals and floating holographic displays. She began the laborious task of cataloging the deviations, cross-referencing with preserved logs, and annotating each invented detail.

Her fingers hovered over a virtual keyboard. She could preserve the original text, annotate it carefully, even attempt to guide the children's stories back to Earth's memory. But the thought carried a quiet futility. Each correction would be temporary. Each child would inevitably reshape the tales again.

She scrolled through an old recording: a history lesson about early space travel, the first steps on the Moon, the exploration of Mars itself. The footage flickered softly, and the sound of distant instructors from Earth echoed faintly. She noticed the youngest children had already misinterpreted the sequence of events. Neil Armstrong became a girl, the Moon landing a playground game. The robots that surveyed Mars were now friendly animals guiding explorers through the desert.

The absurdity made her lips twitch, though it was not amusement. It was a mixture of sorrow and awe. Humans would survive, she realized, but the past would not. History was already becoming myth.

Afternoon arrived slowly, carried by the faint hum of life-support systems and the soft illumination of the habitat's overhead lights. Clementine wandered between clusters of children, observing them as they played with words, reshaped Earth's legacy, and laughed at inventions that never existed.

"Iona," she said gently, kneeling beside the girl, "why do you think the astronauts flew in a playground?"

"Because Mars is big, and we're small!" the child replied without hesitation. "And the Moon isn't scary here!"

Clementine exhaled, realizing she could not argue, could not insist, could not reclaim the stories in the way she wanted. Each retelling was an act of survival, each misinterpretation a necessary adaptation. Humanity would endure, but Earth would exist only in fragments, reshaped in imagination, myth, and play.

Her mind wandered to the archives themselves—the carefully cataloged files, the endless streams of logs, the high-fidelity reproductions of Earth's history. For decades, she had believed preservation could safeguard memory, that accuracy was paramount. And yet, she saw now that memory required more than precision; it required attention, care, and interpretation by living humans. Without them, even the most perfect records were meaningless.

As the sol waned, Clementine returned to her desk, weary but not defeated. She began her evening entry in the personal log she maintained, the one document she could write without censoring or correction:

"Humanity persists. The children reshape Earth in stories, in laughter, in their unfiltered imagination. Preservation is partial. Memory is mutable. My role is not to enforce accuracy but to observe, annotate, and protect the act of remembering itself. The past, even when misremembered, continues to guide the present. It is myth, it is history, it is alive, and it is ours."

She leaned back in her chair, letting the silence settle around her. Outside, the weak Martian sun angled across distant ridges, highlighting faint dust swirls. The children's voices echoed softly through the halls, inventing worlds she could never fully control, stories she could never fully preserve.

A faint laugh drifted through the Archives, and Clementine realized it was hers. Not at the accuracy of the children's retellings, not at the history itself, but at the living memory that endured, imperfect and human.

The sol ended. Lights dimmed. Systems hummed. Logs were preserved. Stories were reshaped. Silence did not destroy memory—it allowed it to evolve.

Clementine closed her eyes for a moment, letting the weight of the day settle, a mixture of melancholy, wonder, and quiet acceptance. Humanity survived, and in doing so, redefined itself. Earth was gone. But life, memory, and story—small, fragile, human things—persisted in ways that no signal, no log, no archive could ever fully contain.

And Clementine knew, finally, that this was enough.

# What the children call the sky

Lila Arden crouched at the edge of the playground, the low gravity making her feel heavier in her chest than in her limbs. The cluster of Martian-born children tossed magnetic spheres back and forth, the spheres clinking and spinning lazily in arcs that would have been impossible on Earth. Each movement was deliberate, precise, as if the children had learned to inhabit every inch of their planet's strange, patient pull. Their laughter, high and brittle, echoed faintly against the steel walls, carried by the recycled air and magnified by the emptiness around them.

She had been observing, recording, cataloging, for four sols, but today something was different. Today, the children seemed to sense her presence not as authority, not as an observer, but as a listener. They paused, mid-gesture, mid-laugh, aware that the language they were forming was being watched, assessed, understood.

At first, documenting the evolution of their speech had been mechanical: compare sounds, log deviations, note Earth-derived vocabulary, chart sentence structures. But slowly, the patterns revealed something extraordinary. The children didn't just speak differently—they thought differently. Their words were sculpted by Mars itself. Low gravity softened consonants, recycled air stretched vowels, and the endless red horizon demanded clarity, precision.

A small boy, barely six, paused mid-throw and pointed to the distant horizon. "The sky," he said.

Lila smiled, soft and automatic. "Yes. The sky," she echoed.

"No," he said, shaking his head with careful insistence. "That's the veil. The sky is behind it. You can't touch it here."

Lila's pen froze mid-air. The correction was subtle, logical, and profoundly alien. The children had learned early: Mars defined their boundaries, and their words reflected those boundaries. Language had adapted, not out of whim, but out of necessity.

A girl, slightly older, leaned forward and added, "We don't call it Earth anymore. That's just old talk. The veil is real. You can see it. You can't see Earth."

Lila scribbled furiously, heart racing with a mixture of awe and melancholy. The veil. A linguistic invention born of absence, of distance, of impossibility. Earth had faded not because it had died, but because it was irrelevant. Mars demanded its own vocabulary.

The children clustered around a low wall, their tiny hands tracing patterns in the smooth polymer surface, drawing shapes for wind gusts, dust devils, the tilt of sunlight along the northern ridges. Lila crouched with them, careful to keep her pen moving, capturing each sound, each word, each inflection.

One boy suddenly called out: "Lila! Tell us a story!"

Her stomach tightened. Stories were dangerous here. They required shared reference points, grounding in Earth-bound culture. But she had none. All of her inherited tales fell flat in a world that moved differently, thought differently, breathed differently.

"Long ago," she began cautiously, "there was a planet called Earth..."

A chorus of polite interruptions erupted. "We know about Earth," said one, rolling eyes with gentle impatience. "It's old. It's not ours."

"And boring," added another, waving a hand. "Tell us about here. Tell us about the veil. Tell us what we can touch, what moves, what listens."

The children's eyes were bright, insistent. Lila realized with a jolt that Earth was already myth. Not gone. Not destroyed. But irrelevant. The story they demanded was of Mars, of dust, of wind, of light, of movement. The story of their world was theirs to write, and they expected her to be the interpreter, the witness, the translator.

She nodded. "Very well," she said, drawing a slow breath. "The veil is not empty. It breathes. It moves. It listens. And sometimes..." She let the pause stretch. "...it whispers."

The children leaned forward, captivated. Mars had become a storyteller, and Lila its humble chronicler. Each whisper of wind across the playground, each dust particle catching light in the viewport, became a character in a story, a phrase in a language, a punctuation in a living, speaking planet.

Hours passed. Lila scribbled notes while the children invented words, gestures, and rhythms for experiences impossible to translate into Earth terms. One boy coined a word for the faint, almost inaudible sound of settling dust: shyrr. A girl invented glintfall to describe sunlight refracting in suspended particles. Others traced shapes in the dust, naming the tilt of light across ridges, the slow pull of gravity on a tossed sphere.

Every word, every syllable, every invented term was necessary. Mars demanded it. Forget it, and it vanished, ephemeral in the thin atmosphere, never to be recovered. Lila understood, acutely, that she was not just a witness—she was a custodian of a fleeting human moment that would only make sense on Mars.

By late afternoon, she realized something profound. The children's vocabulary no longer referenced Earth. Concepts, objects, even emotions were grounded entirely in Mars. Earth existed only as an abstract idea, a cautionary tale, a ghostly legend to be whispered on solemn occasions.

Her chest tightened. As an adult, she had been trained to preserve culture, to maintain continuity, to protect memory. But here, she was witnessing inevitable erasure, and the erasure felt purposeful, natural, elegant.

A child tugged at her sleeve. "Will the veil hear me?"

Lila bent to their level, careful to meet their earnest eyes. "Perhaps," she whispered. "Or perhaps it only listens when you speak carefully... and mean it."

The child nodded solemnly, then ran back to the others, shouting a word Lila didn't recognize. But she felt it, understood it instinctively—a celebration, a mark of belonging, a declaration that this planet was theirs, fully and irrevocably.

She leaned back, watching as the children clustered, invented new words, argued over meanings, laughed, experimented, and built a language no one from Earth could ever fully grasp. The horizon glimmered faintly, the veil stretching infinitely, dust swirling in soft arcs, sun glittering in suspended particles.

Lila realized that she would never fully inhabit this new linguistic world, never fully grasp these children's perception of life. She was a temporary custodian, a chronicler of a culture already moving beyond her. And yet, she was enough. She was witness. She was recorder. She was acknowledgment.

Mars had not erased humanity. It had quietly rewritten it. The first Martian-born generation would never know Earth as it had been, would never need it. They would call the sky something new, something alive, something utterly their own.

As the artificial sunset dimmed the lights across the habitat, Lila whispered to herself:

"Let them name it what they will. Let them live it. Let them forget."

And in the red horizon, the veil shimmered, indifferent, eternal, and entirely theirs..

## The choice not to choose

Alaric Dune leaned over the central console in the habitat's engineering bay, fingers brushing the cool surface of the interface as he traced the readings. The module smelled faintly of recycled metal and antiseptic—a clean, sharp scent that always reminded him of control, of order. Humming beneath the floor and walls were the systems: air circulation, water recycling, power distribution, the invisible currents of life that carried the colony through its sol. All of it functioned flawlessly, yet Alaric's eyes lingered on a single, minor anomaly: a slight fluctuation in the pressure within one of the secondary oxygen lines.

Not enough to trigger an alarm. Not enough to endanger anyone. But enough to pull at his attention.

He knelt and ran a hand along the tubing, letting his fingers hover over the tiny gauge, feeling the micro-vibrations. His mind cataloged the options: monitor, correct, ignore. Each path seemed equally reasonable. But each carried weight, invisible yet tangible, like the faint tremor of dust that occasionally crept through the habitat's walls.

A soft voice broke his concentration. "You've been staring at that gauge for hours."

Alaric looked up to see Liora, the habitat's communications officer, hovering at the entrance. She leaned lightly against the frame, hair loose, eyes soft with curiosity.

"I can't stop noticing it," he admitted, gesturing at the line. "It's minor. Insignificant. But I can't shake the feeling that—"

"—that ignoring it is wrong?" Liora finished for him, a slight smile playing on her lips. "Alaric, it's a fluctuation. The systems are stable. It's almost poetic how perfectly this colony runs."

He chuckled faintly, but the humor was brittle. "Poetic, yes. But poetry isn't safety. I could act. I could intervene. Or I could... let it be. Let it self-correct."

Liora stepped closer, brushing a lock of hair behind her ear. "And which choice makes you human?"

Alaric didn't answer immediately. He leaned back, letting his eyes follow the subtle light cast by the artificial sun along the gleaming floors. Tiny flecks of dust glimmered, drifting lazily in slow arcs. The habitat was immaculate, efficient, safe, and beautiful in its monotony. There was no urgency, no chaos, no unpredictability. Nothing required heroics, ingenuity, or fear. Yet every fiber of his being strained against the perfection, the stillness.

He walked along the narrow corridor connecting the oxygen line to the maintenance hub, hands trailing along the smooth walls. The children passed him occasionally, floating with small, improvised routines, bouncing gently as if gravity were a thought rather than a law. Their laughter, muted yet vibrant, echoed softly against the metal walls. Alaric felt a pang—this life was thriving, yet untouched by challenge, untouched by consequence.

He reached the line again and crouched, letting his fingers brush the gauge. The numbers flickered slightly. There was no failure, no risk, only potential. It was enough to demand a choice, and yet no choice was truly required.

He imagined the options. Immediate intervention: open valves, adjust regulators, reroute pressure. A simple set of commands, precise and predictable. Safe. Correct. Perhaps even necessary in another time, another place.

Or... inaction. Observe. Let the system correct itself. A gamble? Perhaps. A moral test? Definitely. The faintest smile touched his lips. It was absurd, in a way, that survival here demanded nothing. Yet here he was, weighed down by a choice that meant nothing—or everything.

Afternoon sunlight filtered through the viewport, casting long, thin shafts across the maintenance bay. Dust motes twirled like tiny dancers in the air currents, visible only in the streaks of light. Alaric watched them for a moment, letting their small, patient motions mirror the colony itself: alive, persistent, unhurried, and indifferent.

A soft clatter drew his attention. Two of the older children, experimenting with tools in the engineering practice module, were floating small metal parts, testing weight and motion. One dropped a piece, and it hovered midair for a fraction of a second before settling. The other laughed, adjusting their trajectory. Alaric's chest tightened. Responsibility wasn't abstract here—it was palpable, flowing through touch, observation, and decision.

He exhaled slowly, letting the tension leave his shoulders. The system would self-correct. Minor deviations like this were expected, designed into the algorithms, anticipated in every simulation. Acting would change nothing, except to mark him as intervening unnecessarily. Not wrong. Not right. Neutral.

Evening approached imperceptibly. The habitat's lights dimmed, following the gentle arc of the artificial sun. Alaric returned to the console, hands hovering over commands, and finally let himself breathe. He tapped a single sequence: a diagnostic sweep, recording the anomaly, but doing nothing more. Observation without interference. Choice without action.

He leaned back in his chair, letting the hum of the systems fill the silence. Outside, faintly red plains stretched endlessly. Dust swirled, light played across ridges, and shadows drifted over distant craters. He could almost imagine the wind shaping the surface in slow arcs, indifferent and infinite.

A voice came through the comms, soft, measured. "All systems are normal. No deviations detected."

Alaric allowed himself a quiet smile. Not satisfaction, not triumph—something subtler. Recognition. He had exercised agency without interference, weighed responsibility without consequence. He had chosen, and in choosing, affirmed his humanity, even in a perfect, unchallenging world.

He closed the console and walked to the viewport. The sun had dipped low, streaking light across the floor in molten bands of orange and red. The children were gathering in small clusters, voices light, experimenting with gravity, tossing small objects, inventing games that depended only on themselves. Laughter rose and fell, a living counterpoint to the hum of systems.

Alaric exhaled again, letting the long day settle behind him. He realized that morality, responsibility, and choice were not dependent on disaster. Even in the absence of crisis, the human heart could strain, worry, consider, and act—or refrain. That tension, that care, was the spark of life here. The systems would never fail. Mars would never punish them. Earth's memory had faded. And yet, humanity persisted through quiet, deliberate choices, through observation, through attention and care.

And for the first time, he understood that survival alone was not enough to define a person. The space between action and inaction—the weight of choice—was where meaning lingered, subtle and unspoken, shaping the people who dwelled here without anyone noticing, without urgency, without applause.

Alaric watched the children's small shadows stretch across the floor as they floated and laughed, improvising games and discovering delight in gravity, in each other, in themselves. He traced his fingers along the viewport, pressing lightly against the cool surface, feeling the faint warmth of the sun behind it.

He whispered, softly, almost to himself:

"Even here, we are responsible. Even here, we are human."

And then he stepped back, leaving the choice not to choose behind, letting the colony move forward in perfect, subtle equilibrium. The anomaly remained minor, unresolved, harmless. And in the quiet that followed, Alaric felt the full, patient weight of humanity—not survival, not perfection, not control—but the awareness of self, the subtle burden and beauty of moral presence.

Outside, the dust swirled, but inside, humans persisted. Thinking. Observing. Choosing, or choosing not to.

And that was enough.

## A Sol without concern

The alarms were silent.

Not because the systems had failed—they were alive, humming, precise—but because there was nothing to alarm anyone about. No fire, no hull breach, no dust storm tearing across the exposed solar arrays. Every monitor, every relay, every automated system operated exactly as intended. It was a perfection so complete it was almost alien.

Captain Sloane Mira reclined in the observation pod, hands folded over her lap, eyes tracing the subtle eddies of Martian dust outside the viewport. The filtered sunlight cast delicate patterns over the red plains, illuminating particles like tiny golden motes suspended in airless eternity. She could feel the pulse of the colony beneath her fingertips: air circulation, hydroponic nutrient flows, structural stress sensors, automated maintenance drones patrolling corridors in synchronized patterns. Each component performed with flawless precision, no hesitation, no error, no deviation.

Her morning briefing had been identical to the day before, and the day before that: check systems, verify logs, simulate emergencies, ensure readiness. She had spent hours—no, entire sols—crafting theoretical disasters. Solar flares of impossible intensity. Habitat depressurizations. Massive dust storms threatening the solar fields. Rogue micro-meteoroid impacts. Each scenario ran through the simulations, and every time the colony responded flawlessly. Protocols executed, alarms triggered, personnel reacted—exactly as trained.

No panic. No improvisation. No need for heroics.

Sloane exhaled slowly. Almost terrifying.

She rose, moving through the narrow corridors, letting her eyes trace the familiar shapes and textures of the habitat. Engineers calibrated sensors, medics checked vital statistics, teachers guided Martian-born children in exercises of low gravity and high curiosity. Lila, the administrator, cataloged sunlight patterns and seasonal shifts across the dome. Somewhere in the entertainment module, Soren Callas' laughter echoed as children attempted improvised jokes, their humor lighter, stranger, and alien to her old Earth memory.

All of it worked. All of it persisted.

And yet, a heavy unease settled in her chest. She had trained for emergencies, for catastrophe, for the moments that demanded humanity's most desperate ingenuity. And now there was nothing.

Mars did not threaten. Earth did not intervene. The colony existed perfectly, efficiently, beautifully—but without need, without urgency, without imperfection. Humanity had survived, yes. But had it truly lived?

Sloane moved toward the maintenance bay. She examined a newly repaired vent, checking its calibration logs. Even the smallest deviation, once, might have mattered. Even the faintest anomaly could have sparked innovation, fear, collaboration, and camaraderie. But all was precise. All was predictable.

A maintenance drone floated past, carrying supplies along a preprogrammed trajectory. Its tiny thrusters whispered against filtered light. She followed it with her gaze, recalling centuries of human history on Earth: accidents that led to invention, mistakes that bred empathy, catastrophes that forged connection. None of that existed here. All of it had been sterilized by perfection.

She tapped commands into the console, creating simulations to prod the colony, to force error. Breaches, power failures, oxygen recycler malfunctions. Each scenario unfolded in the software with flawless execution. Every sensor triggered the correct alarms. Every human acted as instructed.

Nothing went wrong.

Hours passed like this: inspection, simulation, monitoring, recording. Sloane wandered from module to module, noting how efficiently life flowed through the habitat. Engineers moved with quiet concentration, their hands adjusting dials and relays. Medics recorded vitals, noting subtle deviations but finding none. Children ran, floated, experimented with language, gestures, and laughter. Even the plants in hydroponic gardens thrived, leaves glinting under artificial suns, nutrient flows perfectly balanced.

She stopped in the observation pod again. Outside, dust swirled in lazy spirals, indifferent to her contemplation. The weak Martian sun traced its path slowly across ridges, revealing craters and valleys in soft relief. The colony thrived below her, systems and humans in synchronized harmony, yet she felt a strange hollowness. Survival was no longer urgent; it was sterile. Achievement had become invisible.

Sloane opened her personal log, the one sol-long entry she allowed herself each day:

"Humanity persists. The colony survives. Every system responds flawlessly. Every log is clean. We are safe. We are stable.
And yet... we do not live. Mars does not demand. Earth no longer calls. The pulse of danger, the spark of unpredictability, the chaos that shapes memory and identity—all are gone.
Today, there is nothing to fight, nothing to save, nothing to challenge us.

We exist. That is all. And perhaps that is enough. Perhaps that is all we were ever meant to be."

She rose again, moving through the hydroponic corridors. Water dripped quietly, recycled through circuits that measured every particle, every nutrient, every flow. Tiny droplets clung to leaves like suspended gems. She watched as a small child reached out, curious, cautious, touching the greenery. No harm would come; the system prevented it. Yet the act of curiosity was alive, human, fleeting in a world designed to neutralize risk.

At the central habitat dome, she paused to watch Soren teaching humor to a small group. Laughter, improvised, fragile, and precise, rose into the filtered air. These humans had adapted. Culture had mutated. Even joy, once fragile and fleeting, had found new forms in a world indifferent to it.

And still, Sloane felt it: the gap between survival and living, between precision and humanity, between endurance and experience. She walked past engineers calibrating instruments with exacting care, medics logging perfect vitals, teachers guiding perfect routines. Everything was alive—but nothing had the thrill of uncertainty, the rush of improvisation, the spark of crisis.

She tapped the console again, running simulations. Dust storm. Pressure breach. Power cascade. Each test executed perfectly. Humans responded with calm efficiency. No fear. No courage. No errors.

The sun dipped lower, spilling faint gold over red ridges. The habitat's artificial lighting dimmed to mimic sunset, elongating shadows across floors and walls. Children's laughter continued, soft and irregular, shaped by their own improvisation, unaffected by the indifference of the planet. Systems hummed, drones patrolled, and nutrient flows continued. The colony existed, thriving, uninterrupted.

Sloane returned to the observation pod, folding her hands once more. She studied the horizon. Dust swirled like tiny galaxies, the Martian sun traced patient arcs, and humans moved flawlessly beneath her gaze.

And then, with quiet inevitability, she understood. Humanity could endure without struggle, without danger, without error, without urgency. Survival was possible with a perfect routine alone. All else—the improvisation, the fear, the innovation born from chaos—was optional. Perhaps unnecessary. Perhaps already extinct.

She exhaled, softly, long. The last alarm had never rung. The last error had never occurred. The colony persisted. Mars was indifferent. Humanity endured.

And outside, the world continued, perfectly, quietly, forever.

## A Word from the Author:

Thank you, dear Reader.

I hope you enjoyed reading this story as much as I enjoyed writing it.
This is the first of many stories I hope to share with you and I hope you'll check the rest of them out as I publish them.

*Ordinary Days In an Extraordinary Place* was written during the winter break of my plebe (freshman) year at the United States Naval Academy.
I thank my family for their love and support throughout the journey it took to get this book published, and I thank those at the Naval Academy who helped and encouraged me throughout the process.

Very respectfully,
A. J. Zeren
MIDN USN

www.ingramcontent.com/pod-product-compliance
Lightning Source LLC
LaVergne TN
LVHW050935080826
845145LV00004B/1271